ME TWO

Other Avon Camelot Books by
Mary C. Ryan

THE VOICE FROM THE MENDELSOHNS' MAPLE

MARY C. RYAN has written six books for young people including *The Voice In the Mendolsohns' Maple*. She lives in Pittsford, New York.

ME TWO

MARY C. RYAN

Illustrated by Rob Sauber

AN AVON  CAMELOT BOOK

AVON BOOKS
A division of
The Hearst Corporation
1350 Avenue of the Americas
New York, New York 10019

Text copyright © 1991 by Mary C. Ryan
Illustrations copyright © 1991 by Rob Sauber
Published by arrangement with Little, Brown and Company, Inc.
Library of Congress Catalog Card Number: 90-45690
ISBN: 0-380-71826-X
RL: 5.0

First Avon Camelot Printing: July 1993

Printed in the U.S.A.

OPM 10 9 8 7 6 5 4 3 2 1

ACKNOWLEDGMENTS

Thanks to my good friends Margery and Howard
Facklam for unwittingly planting the seed;
and to Norbert Skibinski of the North Tonawanda
(N.Y.) High School language department for his
translations.

ME TWO

1

Argyle socks had class. Wilf admired the way the blue and green diamonds marched around his ankles, which were propped up and crossed on his desk. He tilted back in his chair and wondered if anybody would be wearing argyles in the year 2015.

The world was going to be a totally different place in another twenty-five years or so. Wilf knew that already. For one thing, there'd probably be plenty of robots: robot cashiers at the grocery store, robot garbage trucks to pick up the trash every week, and maybe even something like Robocop, directing traffic on busy street corners and blasting drivers with rays from his laser gun if they didn't follow orders. Not that the drivers would get hurt. They'd be robots, too.

Wilf felt it was important for him to think about the future right now. He didn't want to be too surprised the next time he stepped out of his house. Because after his mother and father took a look at his latest report card, 2015 was going to be about when he'd get ungrounded.

He had the card in his hand now, although he still hadn't found the courage to open it. It had been lying with all the other mail on a small table near the front door when he'd come in from school. It was addressed, as usual, "To the Parents of: Wilfred D. Farkus."

It was Friday afternooon, and for a minute, Wilf had thought about hiding the envelope until after the weekend. He remembered that his father had said something about maybe going fishing tomorrow. And on Sunday, Aunt Julia was coming for dinner. Aunt Julia never showed up without a huge pan of homemade penuche fudge. If his card said what he thought it did, he wouldn't get so much as a smell of any penuche.

But just as he was about to slip it into his jacket pocket, Wilf caught sight of another envelope. It was from the *Reader's Digest* Sweepstakes, and it was empty. That meant his mother had stopped home for lunch and had already seen the mail. Bills from Merganser's Department Store could stay there until they turned yellow. But *Reader's Digest* Sweepstakes certificates went back to the post office five minutes after they arrived. That was so THE FARKUS FAMILY OF 218 WILLOW-RIDGE ROAD, GATESBURG, had a chance to win TEN MILLION DOLLARS! — plus the $50,000 BONUS! if they beat the deadline. Wilf's mother usually returned the eligibility certificates in the "No" envelope, but occasionally she'd order a map or a book with pictures of the pyramids or some such thing. It didn't seem to make much difference to the *Reader's Digest*. She still hadn't won a nickel.

Wilf's father thought the whole idea was a complete waste of time and postage. Wilf tended to agree with him, but down in the bottom drawer of his dresser was a list of things he just might find a use for someday. Like a Porsche.

There was probably some little Egyptian boy mummy inside one of those pyramids, Wilf thought, as he finally eased the flimsy, computer-printed report card out of its envelope. The poor kid had probably been grounded by the pharaoh because he didn't do his hieroglyphics homework. Then everybody just left him there to rot.

There they were. Just as he'd expected. Three C's. (Hooks, his father called them.) And two D's.

On the positive side, it was somewhat of an improvement over the last marking period. That time he'd had three D's.

"What *is* this?" his father had exploded. "You're about as close to failing as you can get. I never got a D in my life." Wilf's mother started to say something, but his father wasn't quite finished. "Well?"

Wilf stared down at the tablecloth.

"Maybe he needs a tutor," his mother managed to slip in.

"I know what he needs, and it isn't a tutor," Wilf's father replied. "The kid isn't stupid, Rosemary. He's lazy. If he was stupid, it would have shown up a long time ago." He turned to Wilf. "You have until April to bring these grades up, young man. Way up — or we're going to be talking Alcatraz around here, understand?"

He paused. Wilf knew what was coming next. He could almost recite it by heart.

"Just wait until you get out in the Real World." His father's voice made capital letters. "Then you'll see what work is."

Wilf didn't want to be in the Real World. He didn't even want to be in Gatesburg East Junior High.

Gatesburg East was a big change from Barrow Elementary School, where he'd gone ever since he first carried his sneaker bag and resting rug into Miss Mosher's kindergarten. Every year after that, he'd had one teacher for every grade. Not at Gatesburg East. Now he had different teachers for math and for English and social studies and French and Life Skills and everything else. Half of the teachers couldn't remember who he was from one day to the next. The halls were filled with so many kids, you could hardly move without bumping into somebody. Wilf had seen a TV show once about the migration of wildebeests in Africa, with millions of animals thundering along in a great cloud of dust. Every wildebeest looked exactly the same as every other wildebeest. That's what Wilf felt like. Just another wildebeest.

At the beginning of school, he'd managed to get a few good marks, mostly because it was all review. Then it got hard. Every night he'd lugged home enough books to build his own pyramid. He'd opened them, too, and looked at the pictures. But in math, the number problems had grown taller and wider and had big long answers that looked like snakes crawling across the paper. He hated English, too. They never let you read good stuff like Stephen King, or anything about wizards or dragons. And in science lab, you had to carve up poor pickled earthworms and find their ten slimy hearts.

Wilf had finally given up paying attention to any of it. He thought maybe he could learn by osmosis instead. That was how food got into the roots of a tree. He remembered that much from sixth grade. A tree didn't study. It just sat there and let the roots soak up what it needed. Wilf let his brain do the soaking up. He took naps during filmstrips. When the teacher was at the blackboard, he stared at the clock on the wall and thought about what was inside and how small gears were connected to bigger gears and wondered who invented gears anyway. Once in a while, he'd even fake a headache so he could lie down on a couch in the nurse's office and keep track of all the different complaints other kids came in with.

If seventh grade was bad, Wilf didn't even want to think about going into eighth. Or what used to be eighth. From what he'd heard from the older kids, it was more like high school. In fact, you actually could take high school courses in eighth, and then you could take college courses in high school, and then, Wilf supposed, be a brain surgeon before you were twenty. Or the president of General Motors.

It was a shame. If everyone would stop getting all bent out of shape about a few dumb letters of the alphabet that a computer printed on pieces of paper every couple of months, Wilf might have enjoyed school. Sometimes it could be very educational. Like that day in the cafeteria when Ben Vestry got a nacho chip stuck in his throat. Ben kept turning rather interesting shades of blue until Mr. Wren, the phys. ed. teacher, walked by. Mr. Wren slapped Ben on the back real hard. The nacho chip flew out and landed on some girl who automatically assumed Ben was starting a food fight. So she whipped the rest of her egg-salad sandwich at him. By the time it was over, Mr. Wren had written up twenty-seven detentions and applied for early retirement.

But now April, which had seemed so far away in January, had spoiled everything by arriving on schedule. Wilf wasn't too sure that changing one D to a hook was going to satisfy his father. In fact, there was about as much chance of that as there was of an iceberg floating down Fowler Avenue in July.

"Wilf! Supper!" His mother's voice came up the stairs, rudely bringing Wilf back to the present. "And don't forget your report card. We're anxious to see it."

Wilf gave one last appreciative glance at his colorful argyles, slid his feet off the desk, and walked over to the window. Tiny new leaves were beginning to stretch themselves out on the limbs of the trees outside. A warm spring sun was slipping behind the houses across the street. In the distance, he could hear kids shouting.

"Good-bye, cruel world," he muttered, and went down to meet his doom.

2

". . . and I can't watch television for the rest of the school year," Wilf shouted, "not even if there's a speech by the president."

"Who'd want to see that?" Chuckie Mounce yanked up the straps of his bulging knapsack and leaned into the wind.

"I might," grunted Wilf to himself. "You never know."

Chuckie groaned. "Three months! That's about sixty episodes of *Galaxy Patrol* you're going to miss."

"Don't remind me. I can't talk on the phone, either, or have anybody over, or go out after supper, or . . ."

But Chuckie wasn't listening. A rather large piece of newspaper had suddenly pounced on him from behind a fire hydrant and wrapped itself around his head.

Wilf turned his back on the wind. His hair was instantly rearranged into the exact reverse of what had just taken him twenty minutes of combing to do. It was easier walking backward, though. He blinked a few times to clear a speck of dust from his left eye, then held up one side of his jacket as a shield so he could see if maybe the wind was starting to swirl around in a funnel. That would be awesome. He'd always wanted to see a tornado up close.

But the sky was filled with fluffy white clouds that raced each other across the bright blue like swimmers in a pool. Wilf let out a disappointed sigh.

"I don't know what everybody expects," he yelled, louder, so Chuckie could hear him through both the wind and the newspaper. "It's not like my family is a bunch of geniuses. We don't sit around discussing acid rain or whether the United States has too many missiles and junk like that. You'd think my parents would be happy that I'm normal, instead of worrying about me getting into college."

The newspaper gave up on Chuckie and tumbled away down the street in search of a new victim. Chuckie tugged at his knapsack again. Wilf could never understand why Chuckie always brought home so many books, but he thought it was a good thing just then, because they were probably all that was keeping him from being blown into the next state.

Wilf wouldn't say Chuckie was small. At least not to

his face. But last summer, when Chuckie had gone with him to the amusement park, the man operating the Firecracker ride wouldn't let Chuckie on because he didn't quite reach the height marker. Wilf also knew for a fact that Chuckie was still wearing the Batman Underoos that they'd both talked their mothers into buying several years ago.

But it didn't really matter what size Chuckie was. Wilf couldn't remember a time when they hadn't been friends. Mrs. Mounce was always asking Wilf if he remembered putting sand in Chuckie's diapers. Wilf didn't. He did remember the Little Lamb Nursery School, however, and how he and Chuckie once had a smearing war with finger paints.

Chuckie leaned over and bellowed in Wilf's ear. "I can't understand why you don't just do some studying once in a while and get everybody off your back."

"Because."

"*What?*" Chuckie yelled.

Wilf was tired of shouting. He stepped into the doorway of Avery Floor Coverings and pulled Chuckie in after him. "Because it doesn't do any good. Look at Ellen Anne Vanderhoofft. She's a nice kid and all that, but she has a 104 average in math, which shouldn't even be possible."

"She did extra credit."

"That's just my point."

"What's your point?"

"Even if you get an absolutely perfect grade, nobody's satisfied. They keep expecting you to do more. There's no end to it. Think, Chuckie — how can you get better than perfect?"

Chuckie thought about it, then shrugged. "All I know is you're grounded and Ellen Anne isn't."

"Oh, no? I'll bet she does about twenty-nine hours of homework every night, just to keep up her 104 average. No, thanks." Wilf peered out of the doorway. "Hey, isn't that your grandmother over there?" A short, plump figure in a maroon sweatsuit was being propelled along the opposite side of the street by the wind.

"Huh? Oh, yeah. She's on a health kick. She has one of those portable tape players and keeps playing 'I Heard It Through the Grapevine' because she thinks she looks like one of those raisin people in the commercials."

Wilf thought it would be neat to be old like Mrs. Mounce, Sr., who had just moved in with the Mounces. Or like his own Grandma and Grandpa Pearson. They were always traveling to Europe or going snorkeling in the Caribbean. When you were old, you didn't have to work anymore and people couldn't tell you what to do or ground you for getting bad grades. You just did whatever you wanted all the time.

There was a high-pitched beep. "We'd better get going," Chuckie said with a glance at his digital alarm wristwatch. "It's 7:52." He started out of the doorway.

"It's a good thing we can see each other at least twice a day."

"Unless I get transferred to a private school," Wilf said.

"They wouldn't do that."

"Don't be too sure. I heard my parents talking about it last night."

Chuckie's eyes almost popped out of his head and rolled off down the sidewalk like marbles.

"Private schools don't have as many kids," Wilf explained. "My mother thinks if the classes were smaller, I'd get a better education."

"But —"

Wilf grinned. "Relax, Chuckie. They can't be serious. My dad would have to own an oil well to be able to afford a private school."

Chuckie sighed in relief. "Yeah," he said shakily, "or win the lottery."

Wilf's stomach gave a sudden lurch.

As soon as he took his seat in Mr. Oldak's social studies class, right after homeroom, Wilf switched one half of his brain to its osmosis setting, and with the other half started writing a book about how he got famous overnight. He wouldn't be famous when he started writing it, of course, but after it was published and everybody rushed to buy it, he would be. He'd be on talk shows and maybe someday have his own Christmas special on TV, or —

"*Mis*-ter Farkus!"

Wilf almost inhaled the pencil he'd been chewing on. He could feel Mr. Oldak's hot breath on his neck.

"Mr. Farkus, would you kindly explain how you trained yourself to read upside down?"

Wilf looked at his book. It *was* upside down. How had that happened? Fortunately his osmosis came to the rescue and he remembered a magazine article about how to use humor to ease a difficult situation. He turned in his seat and raised his arms. "You caught me, Mr. Oldak, sir," he said with a nervous chuckle. "I'm actually an alien from the planet Zorgon. We're light-years ahead of earthlings in intellig —"

Mr. Oldak's hand darted out like the head of a rattlesnake and snatched Wilf's collar. Wilf had to scramble to his feet to avoid being strangled.

Mr. Oldak's face was red. It clashed, Wilf noticed, with the pink button-down he was wearing.

"Then you will be pleased to hear that you have the honor of being Gatesburg East's very first alien — in detention! Got that?"

Wilf tried to nod, but his Adam's apple got hung up on Mr. Oldak's fist.

Mr. Oldak released him so fast, Wilf lost his balance and cracked his shin on the rung of his seat. He rubbed his leg and glanced around. All the other kids were hunched over their books. Everybody but Heather Spears-Croxton, that was. She was looking straight at him, and she was wearing one of the most sickening smiles Wilf had ever seen.

Heather Spears-Croxton scared him. She was tall. Very tall. Scuzzy Shusterman thought she could probably stand up in the shallow end of the school swimming pool without getting her knees wet. Wilf didn't know about that, but he did know she was also bossy. She organized CastleQuest games, which was all right, Wilf supposed, but then she insisted that all the knights be captured by dragons so the princesses could rescue them. She always had ideas for running the school better, which she wrote down and gave to Mr. Stefanec, the principal. Once she even ordered a ninth-grade girl to pick up a tangerine seed that had missed the garbage. Wilf could see how Heather got like that. Her parents. Mr. and Mrs. Spears-Croxton, who were even taller and bossier, were always arguing with the Board of Education over something or other.

Wilf didn't usually pay any attention to Heather, but last Wednesday, Marilee Manzetti had told him that Heather wanted him to be her date for the class dance in June. Wilf didn't have the foggiest idea of what to do about it. He wouldn't have minded so much if it had been Marilee herself who asked him. At least she was normal, and even kind of cute. But he didn't know how to go about changing the situation, and osmosis hadn't been much help in figuring it out, either. He hoped that if he kept quiet, Heather might forget she even asked him. Or Marilee had asked him. Or whatever. It was just one more thing that made his life miserable. Wilf focused on his still upside-down book and wished his father had grounded him from school, too.

"Boy, you sure picked the wrong day to get funny with Oldak," Chuckie remarked after school when Wilf told him he wouldn't be walking home. "Where were you? Everyone in the whole place knew that he totaled his car last night."

"It wasn't on the morning announcements," snapped Wilf.

"Okay, okay," Chuckie said, slipping on his knapsack. "I'll see you tomorrow. I have to go now. The guys are playing Capture the Flag in the field next to Shuster-man's house."

Wilf watched him leave, then gathered up his jacket and books and shuffled to the detention room on the far side of the first floor. He handed in his pink slip to a yawning teacher who didn't seem to be any happier about being there than the twenty or so kids scribbling away at their desks.

Wilf took a seat halfway down the fourth row. It was 2:45. A whole hour to kill. He wished he was playing Capture the Flag out in the fresh spring air. He wished Mr. Oldak hadn't wrecked his car. He wished that some aliens from the planet Zorgon would come and whisk him away in their spaceship.

He fussed around, smoothing out a stack of ditto sheets, until the teacher let out a polite cough and stared down the row at him. Wilf sighed. There was nothing else to do except take a look at his English assignment and hope his osmosis would tell him what to put down.

"Write a paragraph about a famous person whom you admire."

Wilf counted the dots in the ceiling tiles for several minutes. Then he tore a sheet of paper from his notebook, uncapped his erasable pen, and wrote:

Once upon a time, there was a lady named Heather Spears-Croxton, and she married a kid named [Wilf twirled the pen between his fingers and thought hard] Chuckie Whatever-Mounce [he didn't know what the other side of Chuckie's family was called], and then they had a kid named Ralph Spears-Croxton-Whatever-Mounce, and he grew up and got married to a girl with four names, too, and they had a kid, and after that went on for about a century, they ended up with a kid named Stephen Smith-Jones-Randall-Oldak-Brown-Wilson-Washington-Jefferson-Madison-Franklin-Mosher-Edwards-O'Malley-Spears-Croxton-Whatever-Mounce-Manzetti-Stefanec-Shusterman-King, and the first time he had to write his name on his paper, it took him so long that he was too old to go to school anymore. So he never had to study and he became a famous writer and wrote scary books, but they made him shorten his name to just Stephen King so that it would fit on the book cover, and he never had to work again. The End.

3

The first thing Wilf did when he finally got home from school that afternoon was check the mail. On top of a stack of letters was a brightly colored circular about an automatic bed with a built-in television at the foot. Pretty soon they'd have beds with built-in refrigerators and bathrooms, Wilf thought.

The rest of the mail was uninteresting. There was some kind of report from Congressman Honeycutt, a meter card from the water department, and a catalog for women's clothes. Nothing, thank heavens, from the *Reader's Digest*.

Wilf didn't want to admit it, but he was worried. As soon as Chuckie had mentioned the lottery, his mind had immediately jumped to the *Reader's Digest*. What if THE FARKUS FAMILY OF 218 WILLOWRIDGE ROAD, GATESBURG, had TEN MILLION DOLLARS! in the GATESBURG PERMANENT STATE TRUST BANK right this minute? They wouldn't even need the $50,000 BONUS! for beating the deadline. Ten million dollars would send every kid in the Gatesburg East Junior High to a private school — and every one of them would own a Porsche.

As much as Wilf didn't want to be in Gatesburg East, he didn't want to be in any old private school even more. It would be awful to have to go someplace where you didn't know one person. He'd miss all his friends, but especially Chuckie. Without Chuckie, he'd feel like that Egyptian boy mummy left alone to rot in the pyramid.

He couldn't let that happen. But what could he do? He hated to think of it, but there might not be any solution except to take Chuckie's advice and start studying. Although it was probably too late. Even Ellen Anne Vanderhoofft wouldn't be able to cram a whole year's worth of science and math and everything else into three months. He was not going to be able to bring his grades up, and when the first *Reader's Digest* check came, off he'd go.

Wait a minute. He was being ridiculous. Nobody ever won those contests. Nobody he'd ever heard of, anyway. Well, Mr. Burch across the street did get first prize in the Day 'n Night Supermarket's Grand Opening last year. He'd won a year's supply of dog food. Which would have been okay, Wilf supposed, if Mr. Burch had owned a dog.

On the other hand, *somebody* had to win. Wilf had read the tiny print on the back of one of the eligibility certificates. "All prizes will be given away," it said. Just his luck one of them would go to THE FARKUS FAMILY OF 218 WILLOWRIDGE ROAD.

"Anything for me?" His sister, Allana, stood in the doorway of the kitchen, munching on an apple with her black mouth.

Wilf still wasn't used to Allana's "new look." She was fourteen, and if all ninth-grade girls were as strange as she was, maybe he'd be better off flunking so he'd never get there.

A few months ago, Allana had decided that black made her look cool. She already had long, dark hair, which fell straight down from the top of her head like a black waterfall. She wore black clothes, black jewelry, and black mascara. Sometimes, like now, even black lipstick. She reminded Wilf of Morticia on reruns of *The Addams Family*. In fact, that's what he secretly called her: Morticia. He couldn't understand how his parents could let her out in public. They wouldn't allow her to dress like that for school, of course, but everywhere else was okay. Wilf tried to pretend he wasn't even related to her, but it was difficult with a name like Farkus. Just last week, he'd heard his father explaining to Mrs. Nunzio over the back fence that Allana was just going through a stage. As far as Wilf could see, Mrs. Nunzio, who had seven kids of her own, hadn't been too impressed.

Morticia slid into the room like a shadow. "I hear

you're really grounded. Too bad." She could have sounded a little more sincere.

"I'll live," Wilf answered, edging toward the stairs. Morticia gave him goose bumps.

Morticia quickly glanced at Congressman Honeycutt's report and the meter card, took the catalog, and announced that she was going over to her friend Kathlyn's house and would be back by five.

"It's your night for supper," she called back over her shoulder. "Mom left a note on the counter. And don't burn the vegetables." She giggled as the screen door slammed behind her.

Fine, Wilf mumbled to himself. Scorch the creamed corn once in your life, and you never live it down.

Wilf continued up the stairs. Just as he was passing Morticia's room, he heard the muffled ring of the phone from inside. If she ever got grounded, he thought, the phone company would go bankrupt. He hesitated. He wasn't supposed to use the phone, but did that mean he couldn't even answer it? What if his father had had a flat tire and was going to miss supper? What if somebody had spotted a tornado heading this way, and they were calling all the houses to warn people? What if . . .

He stepped into the room. Talk about tornadoes! Every one of Morticia's black clothes, it seemed, had been sucked out of her closet and dresser, thrown into the air, and then dropped. Wilf felt like he was standing in the middle of a coal mine.

Still the phone rang. It was one of those cordless kinds that let you wander around while you talked. Except where was it? Wilf pawed through the clothes. Nothing. He pulled stuff off the bed. The ringing was louder. He almost had it. He lifted the pillow and pounced. Quickly, he slid up the aerial, flicked the switch to "Talk," and yelled into the receiver.

"Hello?"

On the other end, someone hung up.

Wilf threw the phone back on the bed. He hated when that happened.

He was just walking from the room when he spied a paper lying on the floor near Morticia's overflowing wastebasket. MAN SURVIVES FIVE WEEKS ON ROLLER COASTER! screamed the big black headlines. Farther down was a picture of a huge boulder and another caption: NAPOLEON'S AUTOGRAPH FOUND IN CAVE IN ROCKY MOUNTAINS! Both of the stories looked interesting. Wilf liked to read about unusual things. As far as he knew, he wasn't grounded from books and newspapers, so he picked the paper up and went down the hall.

Ten minutes later, Wilf had finished both articles in the *Weekly Screamer*. He felt cheated. The stories were fake. A man had spent five weeks on a roller coaster, all right, but not a moving one. It had been parked in a storage shed for the winter. The man had broken in to get out of the cold. As for Napoleon's autograph, someone had painted *Visit Joe Napoleon's Italian Ice Stand* on the wall of the cave.

How could newspapers get away with lying? Wilf wondered. Wasn't there a law against that? Well, okay, maybe they hadn't exactly *lied,* but they'd sure tried to make him believe one thing when they'd really meant something completely different.

He was about to throw the paper away in disgust, when he caught sight of an ad on the page next to the story about Napoleon's autograph.

Wilf was fascinated. Were there really such things as tiny sea creatures that you could actually train? Or was this just another trick by the *Weekly Screamer*? The ad said "live." He may not have had the best marks in the world, but he did know that "live" meant a thing had life. It wasn't dead. And it wasn't like a rock or a bologna sandwich. "Live" meant a thing could breathe and eat. The OceanPups came with an aquarium and food, so they had to be living creatures.

An idea started taking shape in the back of Wilf's mind. Just last Wednesday, Mrs. Donnally had told the kids in science class that everyone had to complete a project by the end of the year. It could be about anything they'd learned and would be counted as a quarter of their grade. Chuckie was already at work on a model of the digestive system, and Garin Shusterman was growing grass seed on a wet sponge. Wilf had thought about using a cardboard Halloween skeleton and labeling some of the bones, like the skull and ribs and big toe. But this would be even better! It would be so spectacular that he'd probably get an A! Then maybe his parents would stop talking about private schools, and he could stop worrying about the *Reader's Digest* Sweepstakes.

Wilf opened the top drawer of his desk and took out a pair of scissors. Carefully he cut along one side of the order form at the bottom of the ad, then along the other. He slid his left hand underneath to hold the flap of paper and started across the top.

"*Ouch!*" he yelped as the scissors bit into the skin at the top of his index finger. A drop of bright red blood appeared, swelled, and then began to trickle down his finger. He sucked the blood off. Another drop started to form, but it was smaller. Wilf stuck his finger back in his mouth and went to the bathroom to get a bandage.

When he got back, he finished clipping out the OceanPups ad. He printed his name, address, and zip code in the spaces, wrote down the OceanPups order number, and added up the price of the kit, plus postage and handling. He took his plastic *Tyrannosaurus rex* bank down from the bookshelf over his bed, turned the round plastic plug at the bottom, and dumped the money out on the spread. Buying the OceanPups was going to take just about every cent he had: what was left of his birthday money, the two dollars he'd earned helping Garin Shusterman with his paper route for a week, and some change. But if he got an A from Mrs. Donnally, it would be worth it.

There was an old envelope in one of the side drawers of his desk. Wilf addressed it to The Impossibility Company. Then he scooped everything inside: the order form, four dollars and thirteen cents, and, although he didn't know it, a small snip of skin from the index finger of his left hand.

4

The aquarium was ready. Wilf had followed the instructions in his OceanPups kit the night before, adding water to the clear plastic container and dumping in the packet of cleansing crystals. The water had to stand for at least twelve hours so that the OceanPups eggs would be able to hatch properly.

Wilf was excited. His project was really going to get Mrs. Donnally's attention. OceanPups were a heck of a lot more interesting than growing grass on a sponge. Maybe school wasn't so bad after all. For the first time all year, he was actually enjoying himself. And it felt good. Either his father didn't know, or else didn't remember, what it was like to be grounded for so long. He worked for Overman's Safety Equipment and got to drive around all day selling moon suits and masks that made you look like Darth Vader and neat stuff like that. For the past four weeks, Wilf had been constantly stuck with cleaning up the kitchen after supper because Morticia wanted to go and study with her *ghoul*friends. Or with running about a thousand errands to the Day 'n Night Supermarket.

But soon he'd be free. He could almost picture Mrs. Donnally writing that A in her grade book. Maybe she'd even call his parents and let them know what a wonderful job he'd done!

The brown cardboard carton containing his OceanPups kit had been on the doorstep when he'd come home from school the day before. He'd opened it right away and read the instruction booklet from cover to cover. He learned that his OceanPups would come out of eggs that had been around for years. The scientific name for it was *cryptobiosis,* or "hidden life." According to the booklet, one example of cryptobiosis was the grains of wheat from ancient Egyptian tombs. The wheat had sprouted, even after being sealed in airtight containers for centuries.

Wilf also learned that his new pets were a type of brine shrimp, except that you didn't need any knowledge of biology or chemistry to raise them. And they really did do tricks, although they were only reactions to differences in light. There was another big word for that. *Phototaxis.* Wilf felt he was getting more of an education now than he'd ever gotten in all the years he'd been in school. Why, if he kept it up, pretty soon he'd probably have a higher average than Ellen Anne Vanderhoofft.

It was time. Wilf carried the plastic aquarium into the bathroom, just in case the OceanPups got too frisky after being cooped up in those eggs for so long. He tore open the foil package marked "PetPak" and dumped it in. Then he added the "Miracle Growth Food." With the end of one of Morticia's makeup brushes, he gently stirred the water. He peered in through the round bumps on the side of the aquarium that were supposed to be like magnifying glasses. He couldn't see much of anything. Just some tiny specks swirling around.

The phone rang. Wilf went to answer it, closing the bathroom door behind him to shut out any breezes. People with babies always worried about keeping them away from drafts. He didn't want his OceanPups babies to catch cold, either.

As usual, the phone wasn't in its cradle on the kitchen counter. It kept ringing. He finally located it between the cushions of the living-room couch. Wilf was sure the caller would hang up before he got the switch flipped, but he tried anyway.

"Hello?"

"It's me," said Chuckie. "What are you doing?"

"Chuckie, I'm not supposed to use the phone."

"Oh. I forgot."

"For your information, I'm hatching eggs."

"Sure you are. Do you cackle, too?" Chuckie made a gobbling noise.

"Cut it out," Wilf said. "Remember those sea creatures I told you I was sending away for? For my science project? I got them. They're growing right now."

"Yeah? Can I come and watch?"

Wilf thought for a minute. He wasn't supposed to have any of his friends in the house. But he was so excited about his new OceanPups, he wanted to share them with Chuckie. "I guess it'll be okay. I could say you're helping me with my science project. I'll be up in the bathroom. Just walk in."

Wilf switched the phone off, absently set it back between the couch cushions, and went back upstairs. He opened the bathroom door.

And instantly slammed it shut.

5

   Wilf leaned back against the wall opposite the door. He closed his eyes and tried to remember exactly what he'd seen. No. It *couldn't* have been! It was impossible!

He stayed there, breathing in short gasps. After what seemed like forever, he heard the screen door bang and footsteps come up the stairs.

Chuckie laughed when he saw Wilf's face. "Have you been reading *Cujo* again?" One night Wilf had slept over at the Mounces' and had a horrible nightmare that he was being attacked by a giant man-eating dog. It turned out that he was lying on the zipper of his sleeping bag.

Wilf didn't trust his voice just then, so he tried to point in the direction of the bathroom. His hand was shaking so hard, he thought his fingernails might come flying off and pin Chuckie to the wall like the knife-thrower in the circus sideshow.

"Talk to me," Chuckie said, exasperated.

"O-o-o," Wilf stammered.

"And a Merry Christmas to you, too, Santa."

"O-o-open the door." Wilf got it out at last.

Chuckie opened the door.

And slammed it shut.

"This is some kind of a trick, right?" he demanded. Then he grinned. "Oh, I get it. You rigged up a camera in there, didn't you?"

"Chuckie . . . ," Wilf began.

"That's really neat." Chuckie reached out and tugged at Wilf's shirt sleeve as if to reassure himself. "For a minute I thought you'd learned some new kind of ventriloquism."

"Chuckie —" Wilf tried to cut into Chuckie's babbling. "Chuckie, listen to me. It isn't a trick. Not one that I did, anyway."

"Sure. Next you're going to tell me that this is your science project."

"I thought it was. I don't know what happened. It's supposed to be OceanPups in there."

Chuckie looked from Wilf to the door and back again. "Are you sure you followed the directions?"

Wilf found that he could breathe easier now. He knew he wasn't going crazy. Not since Chuckie had seen it, too. Although it could have been a mirage, like when you drove down a road in the summer and saw fake pools of water. "Let's look again," he said to Chuckie. "Maybe it's gone."

Chuckie eased the door open a fraction, put one eye to the crack, then quietly shut the door. "Nope."

Wilf paced nervously up and down the hall. "This is weird, Chuckie. What are we going to do?"

"Do? Why do we have to do anything?"

"Well, we can't ignore it."

"Sure, we can," said Chuckie, reasonably. "Watch." And Chuckie started for the stairs.

"Wait!" Wilf pulled him back.

"I have to get home," Chuckie said. "My mother wants me. I think she said I had to set the table for supper."

Chuckie sounded scared. Wilf was scared, too. "You don't have to do anything," he said. "Just stay outside in the hall, okay? Just in case."

Chuckie gulped, but nodded.

"Okay, then." Wilf put a trembling hand on the door-knob, pushed back the door, and went in.

"Hi," he said uncertainly to the Wilf who was sitting on the toilet seat.

At least he *looked* like Wilf — uh, himself. His Wilf-brown hair was just a bit longer than Wilf's, and he peered at Wilf from Wilf-blue eyes. He also had, as far as Wilf could see, an identical Wilf-body, right down to the small brown mole on the right side of his neck.

The other Wilf tilted his head. Then he said, "Hi," in a Wilf-voice.

"He can *talk!*" cried Chuckie, suddenly appearing behind Wilf. Wilf almost jumped right out of his skin.

"He can *talk!*" cried the other Wilf.

"What's your name?" asked the first Wilf.

"What's your name?" asked the other Wilf.

"I'm Wilf," said the first Wilf.

"I'm Wilf," said the other Wilf.

Wilf bristled. "You are not!"

"You are —" began the other Wilf, but Chuckie broke in.

"Shush!" Chuckie put his finger over the other Wilf's mouth. "Be quiet." The other Wilf put *his* finger over Chuckie's mouth. Chuckie brushed it aside. "Stop it. Now, just listen." Chuckie seemed braver now that he saw nothing terrible was about to happen. He turned to Wilf — the first Wilf — and said, "Did your parents ever say anything about a twin brother?"

"Sure, Chuckie. They've kept him hidden in the basement for twelve years. Get serious, will you?"

"Have you got a better explanation? This guy looks more like you than you do."

"Well, he's not my twin brother, so you can just forget that idea."

Chuckie thought some more. "Then maybe he's from outer space. Like E.T. He sounds like he's trying to learn our language."

Wilf remembered the day he'd told Mr. Oldak he was from the planet Zorgon. He'd been trying to make a joke. It didn't seem very funny just now. "What if he is? How'd he get here?"

Chuckie shrugged. "Did you check the lawn for flying saucers?"

Wilf shook his head. "I don't think he's an alien," he

said slowly. "This is going to sound really dumb, Chuckie, but I think he came out of that OceanPups kit." He picked up the empty aluminum-foil packet that lay crumpled on the floor.

"Sure," Chuckie said with a sneer. "You nut! His *toenail* wouldn't even fit in there!"

"I don't mean that. I mean, he *hatched!* From an OceanPups egg."

Chuckie snorted. "Your imagination didn't just run away with you, Wilf. It galloped! They don't freeze-dry people, like — like *instant coffee,* for cripe's sake!"

Wilf didn't feel like arguing just then. It wasn't really all that important where the other Wilf came from. "What are we going to do with him?" he asked Chuckie.

"He's going to catch pneumonia and solve the whole problem, if we don't get some clothes on him," Chuckie said. He grabbed a bath towel and wrapped it around the other Wilf's waist, tucking the end in to keep it on. The other Wilf put his arms around Chuckie's waist. "Cut that out!" Chuckie said sternly.

"Wilf? Are you home?"

Wilf went white. "It's my sister!" he hissed.

Morticia's voice came up the stairs. "I'm going to start supper. I hope you remembered to take the ground beef out of the freezer. If you didn't, you're dead meat!" Wilf could hear her snickering at her own joke.

"What's with her?" whispered Chuckie.

"Quick!" Wilf took the other Wilf by the hand. "We

have to get him out of here." If Morticia ever got wind of this, the whole world would know about it in three minutes. "We've got to hide him, Chuckie. At least until we can figure something out. You're the one who was talking about E.T. Remember what almost happened to him?"

6

Wilf's radio was still blaring music from the rock station he'd been listening to earlier. Wilf turned down the volume so he could think.

"Clothes," he mumbled to himself. "I have to find some clothes." His room wasn't a coal mine like Morticia's, but it wasn't exactly neat, either. On the chair in front of his desk was a pile of shirts and pants that hadn't been clean enough to put back in his dresser or dirty enough to put in the wash. On the top, Wilf found a green-and-white-striped rugby shirt and a pair of jeans. Then he took some underwear from his dresser.

Chuckie and the other Wilf were sitting on the bed. The other Wilf was listening to the radio. His head was bobbing up and down, and he was tapping one bare foot silently on the floor. The song that was playing just then was one of Wilf's favorites.

"Here, get these on him," Wilf said, tossing Chuckie the clothes. "I'll see if I can find some sneakers."

The floor of his closet was somewhere underneath the sports equipment and other junk he didn't have room for on his shelves. And somewhere on that floor were his old Athletix sneakers, the ones he used when he didn't want to get his good ones muddy. Only where? Wilf burrowed deeper and deeper. He'd just located the end of what seemed to be a shoelace, when he heard a sound that made him freeze. The sound of a door opening.

Wilf peered through the crack in the half-opened closet door. Morticia! His sister was standing over the other Wilf, who was still sitting on the bed, but who now, thank heavens, was wearing the shirt and pants.

"So, taking a pound of ground beef out of the freezer is beneath your dignity, right?" she demanded. "Just who do you think you are, anyway?"

"I'm Wilf," replied the other Wilf. Suddenly he jumped up and began twisting his body in time to the music. "Hey, baby, let's get down! This is the Boogie Man from WROK. We've got what's hot and we're gonna boogie 'til we drop."

Morticia stared at him. "Spare me. We'll see how cute you are when Mom and Dad get home." With that, she spun on her heel and left.

"What's with her?" the other Wilf whispered.

Cautiously, Wilf crept out of the closet, checked the

hallway to make sure that Morticia had gone, and then closed the door. He dumped the rest of the clothes off his chair and jammed it under the doorknob.

"Wow!" Chuckie was gaping at the other Wilf. "Did you hear him? He didn't repeat anything this time. He talked, just like he was normal!"

Wilf wasn't paying any attention. His mind was too busy trying to understand what had happened. Something had gone terribly wrong with his science project. All he'd wanted to do was to grow OceanPups. The instruction book didn't say what you should do if you got a person instead! And not just any person, either.

But what if Chuckie was right? What if he really was a twin and nobody had ever told him? What if his parents had given this other Wilf up for adoption when they were just babies, and now he wanted to come back and find his real mother and father? There were a lot of after-school movies about things like that.

But that didn't explain why the other Wilf had picked just that moment to come back, or how he got in the bathroom, or why he was having so much trouble talking. No, there had to be another answer, and the more Wilf thought about it, the more he was certain it was connected with the OceanPups kit. It was just too coincidental. He remembered there was a number in the instruction booklet to call if you had a problem. Wilf supposed this could be considered a problem.

"I'll be right back," he told Chuckie. "Keep the chair under the doorknob and don't let anybody in, understand?"

Chuckie nodded.

"Spare me," said the other Wilf.

Wilf picked up the OceanPups booklet from his nightstand and stuck it in his back pocket. Then slowly he opened the door and tiptoed down the hall to Allana's room.

Luck was finally with him. Morticia had already changed, leaving her school clothes strewn on the floor and the phone on top of her clock radio. Wilf grabbed the phone and scurried to the bathroom. He locked the door behind him.

The broken pieces of the OceanPups aquarium still lay scattered around on the sink and floor. Wilf picked them up, put them in the wastebasket, and then mopped up the water with a pink-flowered bath towel. If there were any unhatched OceanPups around, they'd have to hang on a little longer.

When he finished cleaning up, Wilf sat on the edge of the tub. He opened the instruction book and looked in the table of contents until he found what he was looking for.

OCEANPUPS HOTLINE: 1-800-555-PUPS

Wilf flicked on the "Talk" switch and pressed the buttons.

It rang six times. Wilf was just about to hang up when a cautious voice answered. "Hello?"

"Is this The Impossibility Company?" Wilf asked.

"Who wants to know?"

"Uh — I do," answered Wilf.

"And who are you?"

Wilf wondered if he had dialed the right number. But before he could ask, he heard scuffling noises on the other end of the receiver and another voice said something that sounded like, "Let *go!*"

"I'm taking care of it," insisted the voice Wilf had been talking to.

"Like you took care of . . ." The words were muffled for several seconds, then Wilf heard something that sounded like, ". . . a *cow* in her kitchen!" and then, "Hello?" asked the other voice. "This is the OceanPups Hotline. How may we help you?"

"Well," began Wilf. "I sent away for one of your kits and —"

"They didn't hatch? That's such a disappointment," the new voice crooned. "We do have a complete guarantee, however, and —"

Wilf broke in. "I didn't exactly get nothing."

"Oh?" There was a brief silence on the other end of the line. "Just what *did* you get?"

"Me," Wilf said simply. Immediately he felt very uncomfortable, and not altogether sure he was doing the right thing.

Another silence. Then the voice cleared its throat. "Ah, perhaps I've misunderstood. Could you possibly be a little more specific about what happened with your kit?"

Before Wilf could begin to explain, however, he heard the first voice pipe up in the background.

"Is it another clone, Victor?"

"Shut *up,* Conrad!"

"I have to go," said Wilf hurriedly. "Nice talking to you."

"Wait!" cried the voice. "Don't hang up!"

Wilf switched the phone to "Off" and broke into a sweat.

7

Back in his room, Wilf waited for the end of the volleyball game that seemed to be going on inside his chest. His head was pounding, too.

A Wilf-laugh came from the floor beside the bed where the other Wilf lay sprawled among a pile of pillows and books. Around his neck was a pair of headphones, which were connected to Wilf's Sony Walkman.

Wilf stared. "What does he think he's doing?"

"Reading," said Chuckie.

"*Reading?*" Wilf momentarily forgot about the strange conversation he'd just had on the phone. "Chuckie, ten minutes ago, the guy was talking like a three-year-old. Are you asking me to believe he's actually *reading?* Wilf bent over and peered at the cover of the thick paperback book in the other Wilf's hands. "*The Lord of the Rings?*"

"He does seem to learn stuff pretty fast. You know," Chuckie went on, "he really might be from outer space. It's almost like he has a computer for a brain."

"Chuckie," Wilf said suddenly, "what do you know about clones?"

"Clones?" Chuckie scratched his head. "Well, Mrs. Wilkins has that collection of African violets on her windowsill. She told us they were all clones of one her mother gave her. She just breaks off a leaf and sticks it in the soil, and after a while it grows into an identical plant. It's like a copy."

"You mean a *Xerox?*"

"Not exactly. But sort of, I guess. Hey, maybe that's what you did — stood too close to your dad's copier." When Wilf didn't laugh at his joke, Chuckie said, "Hey, Wilf, you don't think —"

"I *can't* think," Wilf said. He stepped over the other Wilf on the floor and up onto his bed. From the bookshelf he pulled out the third volume of the *Children's Illustrated Scientific Encyclopedia.* His mother had started buying it, one book at a time, at the Day 'n Night

Supermarket last year, and then stopped after three weeks when she figured out that it was going to cost too much money to complete the set.

There was no entry for *clone*. It should have come somewhere between *clock* and *clothing*, but it didn't. Nothing did.

"Look up *biology*," suggested Chuckie.

It sounded like a good idea. He took down the B volume and flipped the pages. There turned out to be a ton of information on biology. Nearly ten pages. Wilf scanned the article for any mention of clones. Nothing. He closed the book.

"What about the dictionary?" asked Chuckie. "It's got to be somewhere."

Wilf took down his paperback copy of Webster's and blew the dust off it. He used the guide words at the tops of the pages. "Here it is!" he cried, stopping at page 117. He read out loud. " 'Clone: *n*.' "

"That means noun," offered Chuckie, leaning over his shoulder. He pointed. "It says it's from a Greek word meaning 'twig.' "

"Don't you think I know that?" Wilf asked, pulling the book away. Then he continued. " 'An identical duplicate of an organism produced by replacing the nucleus of an unfertilized ovum with the nucleus of a body cell from the organism.' "

"Gee, how'd you do that?" asked Chuckie.

"I didn't do *anything*," replied Wilf, who didn't even

understand half of the words he'd just read. "I was just trying to raise OceanPups. And I sure didn't stick my elbow in a flowerpot."

"Well, this clone nonsense was your harebrained idea in the first place. I don't even know where you came up with it."

So Wilf told him about his call to The Impossibility Company. "The first guy sounded real suspicious, like he didn't want to admit there even was an Impossibility Company. Then he and another guy got into an argument over who was going to talk to me, and then the other guy got on the line. He was real polite and everything, but he kept asking questions, and I started to feel creepy."

"What did you tell him?"

"Nothing. When I heard this other guy say something about clones, I hung up."

"Smart move," said Chuckie.

"Yeah, real smart," muttered Wilf. "But now what do we do?"

Chuckie shrugged. "Unless you're still planning to hand him in for your science project, I think you'd better tell your parents."

Wilf had already been thinking along those lines. It seemed like the logical thing to do. Except if he did, what would happen to the other Wilf? In every science-fiction movie he'd ever seen, *E.T.* included, the government always wanted to get their hands on any alien creatures. Would they consider the other Wilf an alien creature and try to examine him under a microscope, like a pickled earthworm with ten hearts?

The trouble, Wilf realized, was not that there was a strange kid in his room, but that there *wasn't* a strange kid in his room. Already it was evident that he and the boy who looked so much like him, even down to the mole on his neck, had more in common than just their looks. The other Wilf apparently liked the same kind of music as Wilf and, right at this moment, was obviously enjoying one of Wilf's favorite books. Wilf could almost feel himself on a table in some government laboratory, ready to be cut to pieces.

"No," Wilf said. "Telling anybody is definitely out. We're going to have to hide him. At least until we think up a better plan."

Chuckie's head had been nodding up and down, but just then it switched and started moving from side to side. "You can't just let him wander around the house and hope nobody notices him."

"Maybe I can. Chuckie, where's the best place to hide a tree?"

"I don't know," Chuckie said. "How'd we end up talking about trees?"

"In a forest, right?"

"Right. We're going to take this guy out and dump him in a forest."

Wilf let out a sigh. Sometimes he wondered why

Chuckie got better grades than he did, when Chuckie didn't seem to have an awful lot of common sense. "If you hid a tree in a forest, nobody would notice it," he explained, "because all the trees look the same."

"Unless it was a banana tree and you stuck it in with a bunch of evergreens," Chuckie said.

"Well, he isn't a banana tree. Listen, Chuckie. It already worked. Allana was right here talking to him, and she didn't even suspect that it wasn't me."

"That was once, Wilf. It was just lucky you were in the closet."

"This isn't going to be a permanent arrangement," Wilf said. "It's just for a few days. You said he learns fast. We just teach him to stay out of sight. We can tell him people are dangerous — which, for him, they probably are."

"Maybe that forest thing wasn't such a bad idea," Chuckie said. "Or we could take him to the mall and lose him. Let somebody else worry about it. It wouldn't be any skin off your nose."

Wilf looked across the room at the other Wilf. It was like seeing his reflection in a mirror. A shudder went through him. "Actually it might, I think."

8

Wilf could hear Morticia's fire-siren voice, even through the closed door.

"Wilf! Supper!"

Chuckie looked at his watch. "It's almost six o'clock. My mom and dad are going out for dinner. I'd better get home or Grams will start worrying about me."

Wilf was beginning to get nervous. His plan to keep the other Wilf a secret had sounded good when he described it to Chuckie, but now that they were both going to have to leave, he was wondering if it really would work. You might be able to hide a tree in the forest because a tree couldn't move. The other Wilf could. And if he decided to start exploring before they had a chance to teach him to stay out of sight . . .

"Could you just stick around for ten minutes or so?" Wilf asked. "He listens to you."

"What'll I tell him?"

"I don't know." Wilf waved his hand in the direction of his bookshelf. "Give him the other two *Lord of the Rings* books. They ought to keep him busy for a while. If I don't show up at the table right this minute, Allana will start complaining again and I'll be in even worse trouble."

"Can it get any worse?" asked Chuckie.

Wilf ignored that. "You'd better come on over later and help me figure this thing out. We can use the same excuse about you helping with my project. But just in case, set off your wrist alarm under the window and I'll sneak you in the back door." This could really get complicated, with two kids hiding in his room.

"How did school go today, Wilf?" Wilf's mother asked as she passed him the platter of meat loaf.

Wilf had almost forgotten there was such a thing as school, but before he could even take a breath, Morticia jumped in. "He probably did absolutely nothing, the same as he does at home. Honestly, I don't know why you let this child get away with murder. He couldn't even take the ground beef out of the freezer this afternoon. It was like a brick, and I ended up having to nuke it."

"I wish you wouldn't refer to microwaving as nuking, Allana," Wilf's mother said. "Especially with your Aunt Julia a charter member of the Cranston County Coalition for a More Peaceful Tomorrow."

Wilf wished Aunt Julia could talk Morticia into joining the Coalition, too, whatever it was. Maybe that would make some of *his* tomorrows peaceful.

"Your sister Julia could solve the whole problem of nuclear disarmament simply by going into the penuche business full time," Wilf's father said with a chuckle. "Then we'd all be too fat and lazy to go to war."

"That's nothing to joke about," said his mother. "Julia takes her civic duty very seriously. She's volunteered to work for Congressman Honeycutt's campaign for re-election. She said she's in charge of his space platform."

"Far out!" cried Wilf's father.

"Al!"

"Sorry, honey. You made it sound like she's camping on a satellite for the summer."

"She's writing some speeches, that's all. The congressman is very pro—space exploration."

"Wasn't Aunt Julia involved in some protests when she was younger?" asked Morticia.

"Up to her ears," said Wilf's father. "Or wherever. I think she burned her bra on the steps of the county building."

Morticia gasped. Wilf thought back a few years to when his sister had pestered her mother for a bra because all the other girls had them. She probably couldn't imagine anyone burning it after all that hassle.

"Don't listen to him, Allana. He's just being silly. Julia did no such thing," Wilf's mother said.

"She's right," Wilf's father said with a mischievous grin. "Your aunt never even believed in wearing —"

Wilf's mother's hand went over his mouth.

Wilf was glad that the conversation had moved away from him. As it was, he was having a hard enough time keeping his mind focused on his dinner. Just as he'd sliced open his baked potato, he'd seen Chuckie sneak down the stairs and across the hall. Chuckie had flashed him an okay sign with his thumb and forefinger. Nobody at the table had heard the slight click of the front door as he'd gone out. The other Wilf was upstairs — alone. Wilf dug his fork into the steaming white inside of his potato.

"No butter, Wilf? Don't tell me they've got you kids watching your cholesterol, too."

A large piece of potato jumped off the fork and onto his leg. Wilf smiled at his father as he tried to pick up the hot, crumbling chunk with his paper napkin before it burned a hole in his thigh.

"I like it better plain." Wilf managed to get his fork past his chin this time, but now his tongue was on fire. He rolled the potato around and tried to take little breaths of air to cool off the inside of his mouth.

"He's acting weird," Morticia pointed out. "He and Chuckie were up in that room of his all afternoon, and when I went in there to yell at him about the meat, he gave me a whole bunch of some stupid jive talk. He thought he was being cute."

"Science," Wilf blurted out. "It's my science project. I didn't want her to see it. It's a surprise. Gandalf's my partner." He stopped. What was he *saying?*

"Who?" asked his mother.

"Uh — Chuckie. I meant Chuckie. Sure. I didn't think you'd mind him coming in if it was for school. We've got to do a good job on it because it counts a lot toward our grade."

"He could have the whole audience from *Wheel of Fortune* in there for all we'd know," Wilf's father commented, not realizing how close he was to the truth. "I'm not complaining, mind you. Not if you're using your brain for a change, instead of letting it mildew along with everything else in that room."

Wilf's mother flashed her husband a look. "I'm sure Wilf will do a fine job." She smiled at Wilf.

"Why don't you tell us about it?" asked his father.

"Uh —" Wilf thought hard. "Uh, it's a-a-an experiment in — in —" What *was* that word? "Uh, cripfo — no, I mean cryptobiosis. Yeah, that's it. Cryptobiosis. It means 'hidden life.' Like the grains of wheat that were sealed in an Egyptian tomb and then sprouted after they were exposed to air."

There was silence at the table. Wilf's father stared. His mother stared. Morticia stared.

Finally Wilf's father cleared his throat. "Well, that's great, Wilf. Just great." Wilf could tell he was impressed with the big, long word Wilf had learned from his OceanPups handbook. "Sounds like you should be getting an A on that project."

C was more like it, thought Wilf. For *clone*. But out loud he said, "I'm trying, Dad. As a matter of fact, could I please be excused? I just had a big breakthrough before supper, and I want to see how it's going."

Suddenly a thud came from upstairs, almost right over their heads. Then another. And another.

"Your breakthrough sounds like it's breaking through the ceiling," his mother said. "Is somebody up there?"

"It's probably just my schoolbooks," Wilf explained hurriedly. "I wanted to get working as soon as I got home, so I just threw them on my desk. They probably fell off." He got up, rolled his napkin into a ball, put it on his plate, and started out of the kichen.

"I swear there's something going on," he heard Morticia remark as he sprinted up the stairs. "I never heard books fall one at a time like that."

The door to his bedroom was just beginning to open, and a foot that wore an Athletix sneaker was inching out into the hall. Wilf got there just in time.

"You have to stay in here," he hissed in the other Wilf's ear, or whoever's ear it was, and pushed him back. "Didn't Chuckie warn you about people?"

"I hurt," the other Wilf said. He put his hand on his stomach.

Wilf looked at the other Wilf. Could clones get sick? Wilf himself had had the chicken pox once, and several colds. If this Wilf was really identical, did that mean he would have to get the same germs?

The other Wilf raised his nose, sniffing the air.

Then Wilf understood. It had been over three hours since the other Wilf had hatched from the OceanPups egg, or wherever he'd come from. Wilf didn't know many boys his age who could go that long without eating. The other Wilf had to be starved!

9

"I'll have to get you some food," Wilf told the other Wilf.

The other Wilf tilted his head. "Food?"

"Food makes your body work." Wilf was glad his osmosis had managed to soak up a few things. "Now, you stay here. We can't let anybody see you. Remember what Chuckie said."

"Chuckie said they would di-" — he stumbled over the word for a second — "dissect me. What does that mean?"

"It means they'll slice you open so they can see all your guts," Wilf said bluntly.

"Radical."

He'd been listening to too much WROK, Wilf thought, then said, "No, it wouldn't be radical. If you think you hurt now, you definitely would not like a dissection." Wilf pointed to the other Wilf's stomach. "I'm going to get the food in a little while. That will make you stop hurting inside. But you have to promise to keep quiet and not let anybody in, okay?"

"Gotcha."

As he crept back downstairs, Wilf found himself wondering why anybody would ever want to go into the spy business. All this sneaking around and keeping secrets was really getting on his nerves.

His father was standing at the kitchen sink scrubbing the meat-loaf pan with a soap pad. He glanced up as Wilf opened the refrigerator and took out a jar of raspberry jam. "Well, if it isn't the starving scientist. I thought the reason you left half your dinner on your plate was because you were so anxious to get back to your experiment. Personally, if I had fixed that meal, I'd be insulted that you're down here foraging for snacks already. But it was your sister's, and I won't bother to interrupt her with a special bulletin." He winked at Wilf.

Sometimes Wilf didn't understand his father. He could be a lot of fun. He joked around and acted like a kid himself when they went to picnics or ball games. It was too bad that his sense of humor vanished so completely whenever the subject of school or grades came up. But maybe now that he thought Wilf was starting to get serious about things, he'd decided to let up a little.

Wilf got the peanut butter down and started slapping together a couple of sandwiches.

"So, why all the big secrecy about your experiment?" his father asked as he slid the pan back into the drawer beneath the stove.

Wilf fussed around, putting the sandwiches on a plate, while he thought. "Oh," he said, "Mrs. Donnally told us that — uh — that some parents get too involved in their kids' homework, and — and she wanted us to make sure we —"

"I get the picture," his father said. "Remember when you were in third grade and everybody had to make a model house? Robbie Haight's project was only slightly less ornate than Notre Dame Cathedral. Of course, it was probably just coincidence that his father and mother are both architects."

"Yeah, something like that," muttered Wilf, pouring a huge, foamy glass of milk. "Well, back to the grind."

"Go get 'em, tiger," said his father. He took a dishrag and began wiping his hands. Wilf grabbed a handful of chocolate-chip cookies from an open package on top of the counter and escaped.

A look of wonder came over the other Wilf's face as he bit into the sandwich.

"Like this." Wilf made chewing motions with his mouth. The other Wilf imitated him. Then he stuffed in the rest.

"Take it easy," Wilf warned him. "You don't have to make a pig out of yourself." Gosh, he was sounding just like his mother! He broke off half of the second sandwich and showed the other Wilf how to take small bites and then swallow. When the sandwiches were gone, he produced the cookies. The other Wilf had learned exactly what to do. Then he downed the milk in one long, satisfying swallow.

"More," he said.

"Not now," said Wilf. "You have to let your stomach get used to it or you might barf."

"Barf?" asked the other Wilf.

Wilf defined the word.

He was just trying to decide what to do next when the high-pitched beep of Chuckie's watch went off outside his window. Wilf ran down the stairs and through the kitchen to the back door.

"Anybody see him yet?" Chuckie asked.

"No. It's okay if you come in, though. I told them about the project. I just didn't tell them what it was. As long as we keep the door closed, we ought to be safe enough."

"You hope."

"Yeah, I hope." Wilf brushed aside a lock of brown hair that had fallen down over his forehead. Out of the corner of his eye, he could see the other Wilf brush *his* lock of hair aside. "Now, tomorrow's Thursday. You and I have to go to school. Everybody else in the house will be gone, too. We'll have to convince him to stay in the room. I'll see if I can scrounge some extra breakfast, make two lunches, and borrow my mom's mini-TV."

"I've a feeling he's going to get antsy after a while," said Chuckie. "You ought to know what it's like to be grounded. And he didn't even do anything to deserve it."

"He won't know any better."

"But then what? That might work for a day, or even a week. Are you going to keep him here until he's ninety-three?"

Ever since the other Wilf had appeared, Wilf had been trying to think up answers to that question. He hadn't counted on there being so much work involved in hiding him. There were times when Chuckie's idea about leaving him at the mall seemed sensible. But the memory of that strange conversation with the man Victor made him feel creepy again, although he couldn't quite put his finger on why. No, there had to be another solution. He just hadn't thought hard enough.

"We should be able to work it like a math problem," he said finally. "First we get all the numbers, or in this case, the facts. Then we can try different solutions."

Chuckie murmured something about wishing he had a big eraser.

"Now," said Wilf, "what *are* the facts?"

"Him," said Chuckie, pointing at the other Wilf, who had the Sony Walkman plugged into his ears again.

"Okay. We have a kid. He looks just like me. He even acts almost like me."

"Except he has a computer brain," said Chuckie. "Which you definitely don't."

Wilf went on. "We don't really know where he came from, but we suspect it was from the OceanPups kit. Those guys from The Impossibility Company mentioned clones. And from the definition in the dictionary, I'd say that's probably what we have here. Right?"

Chuckie nodded.

"Therefore —" Wilf stopped, defeated. This was one reason he didn't like math. He always knew what the numbers were, but sometimes it got very confusing when he was trying to figure out whether he should add, subtract, multiply, or divide — or all of the above.

"Hey, I feel funny again," called the other Wilf suddenly from across the room.

"Where?" Wilf didn't think he could still be hungry.

"Here." The other Wilf pointed, then started jiggling up and down.

"Oh, my gosh!" Chuckie said. "He has to go to the *bathroom!*"

10

"He'll have to go by himself," Wilf decided. "I can't take him, and it would look funny if somebody saw both of you go in." He pulled the other Wilf toward the door, whispered in his ear, and then shoved him out into the hall. Then he stood back and crossed his fingers. Also, as much as was possible inside his sneakers, his toes.

Chuckie glued his eye to a crack in the door. Wilf chewed on a knuckle.

"He makes it to the bathroom," Chuckie whispered.

"He closes the door." Chuckie sounded like he was doing a play-by-play for a football game. Then, "Uh-oh."

Wilf's stomach turned upside down. "What?"

"Your mother. She just came up the stairs."

"Where's she going?"

"She turns left. She passes the bathroom. Phew, that was close. No, wait a minute! The bathroom door is opening. He comes out. He stops. He looks around. He sees her."

Wilf almost bit off his finger.

"She doesn't notice him. She goes to a closet. She takes out some — yes, it looks like sheets. She shuts the closet door." Then Chuckie gasped.

"*What!*" Wilf had once wondered if you could whisper a scream. Now he knew you could.

"She turns. She sees him." Chuckie's words were coming faster and faster. "She smiles. He smiles back. She waves. He waves. She goes into her room. He scratches his head. He shrugs his shoulders." Chuckie slumped to the floor. "It's okay. He's coming back."

A few seconds later, the other Wilf was safely inside Wilf's room again.

"That feels better," he said, then added, "I saw a lady."

"We know," said Chuckie.

"I didn't talk to her, just like you told me. But she wouldn't cut my guts out, would she?"

"That was my mother," said Wilf.

"My mother," repeated the other Wilf.

"No, not —" began Wilf, then paused, not altogether sure that *his* mother wasn't the other Wilf's mother, too. His head was starting to spin. "Look," he said desperately, "do you know where you came from?"

"Came from? Why? I'm here."

"I mean before," said Wilf.

"Before what?"

"This isn't doing any good," said Chuckie. "If he really did hatch out of that OceanPups egg, he wouldn't have any idea of 'before.' He'd be almost like a baby."

Once Wilf had tried to remember what it had been like being a baby. The earliest thing he could think of was banging his thumb with a hammer when he was two or three. The nail had turned black and fallen off. He'd been terrified that his whole body was falling apart.

"Never mind. Chuckie and I will take care of everything," he said to the other Wilf. "You'll just have to trust us that it's dangerous for anybody else — *anybody* — to see you until we're ready. You're going to have to hide in here while we're at school."

"School," repeated the other Wilf. "Work. Detention." His eyebrows crinkled. "Alcatraz."

"What have you been telling him, Chuckie?" asked Wilf, although they sounded like the words he'd have chosen, too.

"Nothing. It's where you learn things," Chuckie told the other Wilf. "Well, *some* people do," he said with a look at Wilf himself.

"Cut it out," growled Wilf.

"I've learned a lot already," said the other Wilf. "Listen. 'A task force of international scientists today declared war on the so-called greenhouse effect. In a joint statement issued in Oslo, Norway, scientists from seventeen countries said the threat to Earth's environment will only be erased with the cooperation of all countries and asked for strict energy conservation measures to reduce the amount of chlorofluorocarbons released into the atmosphere.' "

"Now why can't you do that?" Chuckie said to Wilf. "Oldak would love it."

"I don't have microchips inside my skull," said Wilf. "Now," he said to the other Wilf, "will you promise to stay out of sight? If you can't do that, we might as well tell everybody and get this over with right now."

"Oh, all right," sighed the other Wilf. "But get your brains in gear, will you? I'm going to have to get out of here soon and do some serious boogyin', man."

"Spare me," sighed Wilf.

11

After Chuckie left, Wilf walked back to the living room. His mother was doing the crossword puzzle in the *Gatesburg Gazette,* and his father was on the

60 •

couch watching television, although Wilf noticed that his eyes were closed.

"Good night, Mom," he said.

His mother put down the paper. "Bed already?"

"It's been a long day," Wilf replied honestly, fighting off a sudden, overwhelming urge to lie down on the floor right then and there.

"You do look pretty tired. Your father and I were just talking about how pleased we are that you're starting to tackle your responsibilities at school. I knew you'd hit your stride one of these days. How's the experiment coming?"

"Oh . . . interesting," he said.

"I'd ask you more about it, but science never was my subject. I'm afraid I wouldn't understand anything."

That would make two of us, thought Wilf, turning to leave.

"Wilf?"

Wilf stopped.

His mother tilted her head and eyed him. "That's funny. When I saw you in the hall earlier, it looked like you could use a haircut. It must have been the light. Anyway, what I wanted to mention was that I know the weather's getting warmer, but try not to change your clothes every five minutes like you seem to be doing tonight. It makes it hard to keep up with the wash. Okay?"

Wilf could feel the back of his neck grow damp. In

a way, it was a relief that even with longer hair and different clothes, the other Wilf hadn't aroused suspicion. Yet. But he couldn't be sure there wouldn't be any more accidental meetings, so he'd have to remember to trim the other Wilf's hair. As for clothes, well, he had enough pairs of jeans for the two of them. All his shirts had different patterns, but there was a pile of white T-shirts in his dresser. That might do the trick.

Wilf went into the kitchen and searched the cupboards. He found a half-empty box of granola bars that had been sitting there since at least March. He put two of them in his pocket, then took a bottle of Wunder Diet Cola from a carton in the corner by the wastebasket.

"You better not."

Wilf hadn't heard his sister slip into the kitchen. He stared at her. The hair around her face had been put into long, skinny braids with colored plastic beads on the ends. They rattled when she moved her head.

"Why not?" he asked.

"Mom's trying to lose weight. She says she doesn't fit in her bathing suit anymore."

Wilf put the bottle back.

"So, I hear you have a date for the seventh-grade dance," Morticia said.

"Who told you that?"

"Monica Manzetti. Her little sister, Marilee, said she helped fix you up." She snickered. "I almost fell over. I figured you thought girls were just boys who wore pink sneakers."

Wilf sighed. Apparently the news that he was going to the dance with Heather Spears-Croxton was all over school. He still hadn't been able to think of a way to get out of it. He'd had a few other things on his mind lately.

Morticia's mouth opened in a yawn. "I need some sleep. Kathlyn and I are trying out for *Macbeth* after school tomorrow."

"What's that? A new kind of hamburger?" asked Wilf.

"Very funny. It's a play, dummy. Haven't you ever heard of William Shakespeare?"

Wilf had. He knew he was going to have to study Shakespeare someday in school. He wasn't looking forward to it. Maybe by the time he got to ninth grade, the Board of Education would realize that writers like Stephen King were important, too.

"We want the parts of the witches," Morticia went on. "I'll need to borrow your black sweatshirt, so I can really get into my character, you know." She started for the stairs.

Wilf's heart used his stomach for a trampoline and ended up in his throat. "Don't!" he croaked.

She turned. "Don't what?"

Frantically, Wilf racked his brains. "Don't —" he said again, "uh — don't forget to lock up. You're the last one in."

"Spare me," she sighed again, but went toward the front door.

Wilf raced to his room.

The other Wilf was asleep on the bed, a funny-sounding half snore/half snort coming from his mouth. Wilf wondered if *he* made the same noise when *he* slept. He grabbed the black sweatshirt off the shelf in his closet and dashed to the door. He stuck his arm out and passed it to Morticia just as she was reaching for the knob. She took it and walked off down the hall mumbling witchy-sounding words under her breath.

Wilf was tired. He wanted to go to sleep. But the other Wilf was on his bed. He must be exhausted after growing from an OceanPups egg into a twelve-year-old, Wilf thought. He took his NFL blanket off the bottom of the bed and covered the other Wilf up. Then he got his sleeping bag out of the closet and turned out the light. Sliding into the bag, he lay down on the floor and wriggled under the bed, just in case his parents should decide to look in.

Dust balls tickled his nose. There was also a lump under his left shoulder. Wilf felt around. It was a rolled-up sock. Wilf used it to wipe the floor around his head.

Settling down, he looked out into the room. It was an interesting view, especially now that it was night. Pale moonlight stretched in the window and made the outline of a trapezoid in front of his desk. Wilf wondered if the outline of the window would be called a shadow, or if the shadow was the dark part of the room. His osmosis was still working on the problem when the door creaked open slightly. Wilf stiffened as his mother's feet went by just inches from his nose.

"You forgot your good-night kiss," he heard her whisper.

Please, *please,* be too tired from growing, Wilf prayed.

The snore/snort went on uninterrupted. His mother's footsteps began to fade. Wilf bunched up part of his sleeping bag into a pillow, stuck it under his head, and tried to sleep. It wasn't very difficult.

12

Wilf sat up suddenly, cracking his head on a bed slat. He lay back down, rubbed his head, and tried to remember where he was. And also why. He groaned. The dream he'd been having about the other Wilf being a dream had actually been a dream after all. He rolled out from under the bed, untangled himself from his sleeping bag, and stood up. The other Wilf's eyes were open.

"Let's dash on down to Don's for a Hearty-Hero, made with all-natural white turkey meat," he said.

"Yeah, just a minute," grumbled Wilf. He'd forgotten to set the alarm on his clock, and the hands showed that he was almost fifteen minutes later than usual. There wouldn't be time for a shower. He grabbed a white T-shirt, a pair of jeans, and his sneakers, dressed quickly, then went out into the hall and checked the bedrooms. Everyone was downstairs. He used the bathroom and stood an uneasy guard at the top of the stairs while the other Wilf did the same. The extra set of clothes had already been laid out on the bed. Wilf gave the other Wilf the two granola bars he'd put in his pocket the night before and told him not to walk around.

The whole family was in the kitchen. His father had one hand on his briefcase while he blew on the steaming cup of coffee he held in the other. Morticia, her spoon suspended over a half-eaten bowl of Sugar Oatsies, muttered spells off into space.

Wilf's mother was gazing mournfully at a slice of bread that was so thin, Wilf thought he could see the pattern of the plate underneath. A glass of watery skim milk stood nearby.

Wilf poured himself a bowl of Oatsies.

"What's that in your hair?" asked Morticia, suddenly breaking off in mid-chant.

Wilf's mother reached over and plucked off a large, fuzzy ball from his head. "Dust," she said. "I know we have a privacy agreement in this house, but I suspect that room of yours might be getting a little out of hand. Maybe we should spend an hour or two tomorrow and go over your clothes. There are probably some things you've outgrown. If we package them up for the Salvation Army, you'll have more space."

Several Oatsies came to an abrupt halt on their way

down to Wilf's stomach. "Not tomorrow," he croaked. He took a sip of orange juice and rushed on. "I mean, tomorrow would definitely not be a good day for that. Chuckie and I are still working on our science experiment. I wouldn't want it to get all screwed up and get a bad mark in science. Again," he added.

"If he's growing stuff in there, it's probably all green and smelly," observed Morticia, wrinkling her nose.

"There's an old saying about people who live in glass houses," began her father.

Morticia raised her eyebrows in one of her "spare me" looks, unhooked her purse from the back of her chair, and left the room.

Wilf had to make sure he was the last one out of the house. He kept finding excuses like forgetting his lunch and needing an eraser and searching for his gym shorts until his mother finally gave up and told him to just lock the front door on his way out. As soon as he heard her car start up, Wilf quickly fixed another bowl of Oatsies and a glass of juice. He carried them upstairs. The other Wilf was standing at the window, waving.

"What are you *doing?*"

"This." He flapped his hand at Wilf, then leaned out the window and waved again as Wilf heard his mother's car beep and drive off. Then he turned and caught sight of the cereal bowl. "Barf."

"Food," Wilf corrected. He knew he only had a few minutes before Chuckie would be along. "You have to stay here," he told the other Wilf, after he'd hooked up his mother's little television and showed him how to use it. "I guess it would be all right if you looked around the house a little bit, but don't touch anything. And if anybody calls on the telephone —"

"Huh?"

"The telephone. It's —" He never realized how hard it was to describe things to people who'd never seen them. "Never mind. I'll show you later. But be careful. Remember the dissection. I was going to fix you a lunch, but I didn't have time. There's some in the refrig — uh, in a big cold box downstairs. You could sneak down later if you think it's safe, but stay here as much as possible, okay?"

The other Wilf nodded his head.

"I have to go now."

"Have a superspectacular, out-of-sight day," said the other Wilf.

Definitely too much WROK, decided Wilf.

School that day was not difficult or boring or even educational. It was sheer torture. Wilf had no time to concentrate on how clock gears worked, or what symptoms he could develop in order to spend a period or two in the health office. Not a minute went by when he wasn't worrying. As soon as the first bell had rung for homeroom, he'd suddenly remembered that his mother sometimes stopped home for lunch. Then during second period, a police car went screaming down Fowler Avenue, red lights flashing. Wilf was sure the other Wilf had been discovered. After that, every time the loudspeakers crackled, Wilf jumped in his seat, fully expecting to hear his name. He suspected that this might turn out to be the longest day in the history of school days. Every second seemed like an hour.

Wilf was careful not to hold any books upside down or do anything else that might get him in trouble. He'd lucked out with Morticia having to stay after school for the witch auditions, but he couldn't afford to spend any time in detention.

Finally it was noon. Chuckie was already in the cafeteria. He waved his Sloppy Joe sandwich at Wilf from an empty table in the back corner.

"Did you get any ideas?" he asked as Wilf joined him. "I mean, about" — he glanced around the cafeteria, then silently mouthed the words — "you-know-who?"

"No," answered Wilf glumly.

"I read an article in the newspaper last night about these parents who locked their kid in his room for eight years. They got sent to jail." He popped a potato chip into his mouth and crunched it.

"But we can't just let him out, either, Chuckie," protested Wilf. "He's — he's different, remember?"

"Why is he so different? He's just like you, isn't he?"

"No! Well, yes, in a way, but —" Wilf buried his head in his hands. He couldn't explain it. He knew that he was a human being. He'd been born to a human mother and a human father. As far as he could tell, the other Wilf had hatched. *His* mother and father had been shrimp!

Wilf's brain couldn't handle it all. The harder he tried to understand what was going on, the more confused he became. Then, "Thar she blows," he heard Chuckie say. He looked up. Heather Spears-Croxton was heading in their direction. If he was going to have problems, Wilf thought, the least they could do would be to take turns.

Heather slid in beside him on the bench. "The dance is three weeks from tomorrow," she said. "I have my dress already."

Wilf didn't know what to say. He still hadn't technically agreed to go to the dance with Heather. She seemed to think the whole thing was set, though, and he didn't know how to tell her it wasn't — without possibly ending up with a picket line of seventh-grade girls marching around his house.

"It's lemon yellow," she went on.

Wilf could feel his mouth pucker.

"I heard you don't have a date for the dance, Chuckie," she said. "Neither does Marilee. Go ask her."

"No, thanks," said Chuckie. "I can't dance."

"I can't, either," said Wilf, hopefully.

Heather looked him straight in the eye. "I'll teach you."

*　　*　　*

After school, Chuckie stayed for intramural soccer in the gym with some other seventh graders. Without him, the walk home was lonely. All of Wilf's worries about school and Heather and the other Wilf were so jumbled up that he couldn't think straight. He tried to focus on other things. He noticed that the city street department crew had fixed the gigantic pothole on Fowler Avenue that had almost swallowed a motorcycle a few weeks ago. There was also a garage sale near the corner of Greenwood, and as he rounded the corner onto Willowridge, he noticed an old, rusty black pickup truck parked at the curb diagonally across from his house in front of the Lougens'. But there was no sign of the police or ambulances or official-looking government cars at 218. Best of all, the mail was still in the mailbox. One of the envelopes was from the *Reader's Digest*, but it was just another sweepstakes. Wilf put all the envelopes on the small table, then tiptoed up the stairs and pushed open his bedroom door. The other Wilf was sitting on the floor, his eyes glued on the mini-TV.

"Irwin's back," he greeted Wilf. "They found him shipwrecked on an island, but Irene told him she's married to Trent now and he should just go and buy another boat, and Irwin says he's going to beat up Trent." He turned the set off.

Soap operas. Wilf breathed a sigh of relief. He'd made it through one day. He closed the door, propped his chair under the doorknob, then kicked off his sneakers and flopped on the bed.

The other Wilf frowned. "I think I've got birds in my stomach."

"Butterflies," said Wilf automatically. He'd been having plenty of them himself, although he had a legitimate reason for feeling nervous. What could the other Wilf be worried about? He'd probably just eaten some leftover that had been sitting around in the refrigerator for three weeks.

"I think I need some fresh air," the other Wilf announced. He pointed to the window. "I want to go out and see people. I'm not exactly having the time of my life cooped up in here, you know."

Wilf wondered how the other Wilf could even expect to have the time of his life when he'd hardly had much life in the first place. The last thing he needed was to have to listen to more grumbling. Especially after the day he'd had.

"Quit crabbing," he said. "You've got it made. You don't have to listen to people yakking at you all day and expecting you to do weird things like multiplying parts of a pie, or prick yourself trying to sew a button on a shirt. You get to sit around and watch television. You're so lucky, it's sickening."

The other Wilf rose from the floor, hands on his hips. "Oh yeah? Well, if you think it's so great, maybe *you* should stay home and let *me* go to school."

And the minute he heard them, Wilf knew they were probably the most important words ever uttered, at least since Abraham Lincoln's Gettysburg Address.

13

Wilf paced the floor, muttering. "Maybe . . . If . . . But . . ."

The other Wilf watched him. "What are you talking about?"

"Nothing. Everything. Oh, I don't know. I have to think about it some more."

Suddenly there was a clicking noise, and Wilf saw the doorknob turn. The legs of the chair that was barricading the door started to slip backward. With one bound, he flew across the room and jammed his shoulder against the chair just as a small crack appeared. Frantically he waved at the other Wilf to stand back out of the way.

"Nobody can come in!" he yelled.

"I promise never to reveal what I've seen, even if they threaten to take away my credit cards," drawled a voice.

It was not Morticia, as he'd feared, but his father — which was worse. Wilf turned pale. The other Wilf tapped him on the shoulder, pointed to the bed, then got down on his knees and crept under. Wilf took a deep breath, tried to relax, and opened the door.

"Hi, Dad. What are you doing home so early?" he said, smiling brightly, although underneath his shirt a drop of cold sweat was trickling with agonizing slowness down his side, one rib at a time.

"It was such a great day, I decided to take a couple of hours off and play a round of golf. I just stopped by to change my clothes. I also wanted to call Ralph Wickerson, only I couldn't find the phone, but then what else is new? I heard voices in here and thought I'd just see if by some strange coincidence —"

"Uh, oh, that was just me, working on my experiment," Wilf said with a little laugh. "Yes, sir. Just me and my old cryptobiosis."

Wilf's father's eyes swept the room. "That's right. I forgot you'd turned this into Dr. Frankenstein's lab. Where is it?"

Wilf fumbled for an answer. "It's under the bed. It has to be kept in the dark. If you look now, you'll spoil the whole thing." Wilf was beginning to think he should apply for a job with the *Weekly Screamer*.

"Next thing you know, we'll have to get top-secret clearance from the government to even talk to you," his father grunted.

"Heh, heh," said Wilf. Another drop of sweat started down.

Just as his father was about to leave, Allana came out of her room.

"I just talked to Kathlyn," she announced, as if anyone was interested. "She's coming over. We both got witches' parts. I told her I'd help her with her costume."

"Witches?" asked Wilf's father, relieving her of the portable phone.

"In *Macbeth*. You know. 'Double, double toil and trouble; Fire burn and cauldron bubble.' " Morticia let out a shrill cackle. Wilf held his ears. "We're doing an interpretive version. All the characters get to choose their own costumes and their own way of playing their parts. My witch is going to be sort of New Wave."

"Shakespeare is probably spinning in his casket."

"Hey, they jazzed up *Romeo and Juliet,* didn't they? Mr. Pauly says that's just what *West Side Story* is — only it's set in New York City, instead of Italy."

Wilf wished the two of them would discuss Shakespeare someplace else. Any minute now, the other Wilf could come out from under the bed. Or else go deaf from Morticia's screeching.

"Well, good luck. Oh, and by the way, I just looked in that room of yours, and you might just think of conjuring up a spell for removing clothes from the floor."

"You think that's messy?" demanded Morticia. "Ha! You should see the kitchen! There's cans all over the place with the labels ripped off and milk slopped on the counter and a dish of what looks like hot fudge mixed with mustard."

"Wilf —" began his father.

"It — I mean, I was —" Wilf gave up. "I'll take care of it," he said.

His father and Morticia finally went away. Cautiously Wilf closed the door and propped the chair back under the doorknob.

"Can I come out now?" The other Wilf's voice came from under the bed.

"Yeah, but whisper, will you? That was close. And did you have to make such a mess in the kitchen? Now I have to go and clean it up."

The other Wilf scrambled to his feet. "I couldn't get the tops off the cans. So I just made my own soup." He made a face. "It tasted terrible."

Wilf could imagine.

"Who was that man?" the other Wilf asked.

"My father."

"What does that mean?"

Wilf hesitated. This was a tough question. No wonder parents had a hard time telling their kids about sex. But he couldn't very well start talking about storks, either, so he just said, "My father and mother are grown-up people. They take care of my sister and me. We all live in this house. We're called a family."

"My sister makes too much noise." The other Wilf dug around in his ear with one finger. "If I live here, am I a family, too?"

Wilf didn't answer. Sometimes a pet was considered a member of a family. Would it be the same for a clone? And if so, would you have to buy him Christmas and birthday presents? It was interesting. He wished he could discuss it with his parents. But right now there was a whole new idea swirling around in his head, an idea that could change his whole life. He needed to talk this one over, too.

"Are you *crazy?*" Chuckie's eyes were bugging out again.

They were standing out behind the garage, where the garbage cans were kept. Wilf had arranged to meet him there because he'd been afraid Chuckie would react the way he'd just done. Although Morticia, Kathlyn, and some other weird-looking girl who were inside sitting on the stairs giggling and shrieking probably wouldn't have heard a tornado pass through.

"Just listen for a minute, Chuckie. He looks like me. He talks like me. In fact, there's only one difference, as you pointed out before. He's smarter, and that's the whole beauty of the plan. We send *him* to school instead of *me*."

Chuckie shook his head. "They'd know there was something wrong right away, Wilf. He's never been to school. He couldn't find his way around and he wouldn't recognize any of the other kids. He'd also get straight A's."

"Stop thinking about all the bad parts, will you? I've got it all figured out. He's got a computer brain. Okay. We make use of it. They took class pictures last fall, remember? We show him those. He can just memorize everybody's faces."

Chuckie frowned. "So how does he get around?"

"We draw him a map, of course. And the best part is, Chuckie, that he likes school. At least, he likes to learn things. Nobody will get hurt. After exams are over, I guess we'll probably have to tell somebody about him, but that's nearly a month away. I needed a miracle to get through this year, and it's been dropped right in my lap."

Chuckie was unconvinced. "Okay, he's a computer brain. But that still doesn't mean he's going to know math or social studies or science or language. You take French, too."

"All he has to do is go over my books. No, I mean it, Chuckie. Over the weekend. There'll be plenty of time. He's already finished two volumes of *The Lord of the Rings* in a little more than a day."

In the end, Chuckie agreed that it might be worth a try.

"That's great," Wilf told him. "Because I couldn't do it without you. You're the guy who's going to make it work."

"Me?" squeaked Chuckie.

"Naturally. You'll have to be with him almost every minute. At least for the first day or two. There's bound to be a few slipups, and since we have most of our classes together, I'm counting on you to cover them up."

"Wilf," Chuckie began, and Wilf knew he was thinking about the mall again.

"It'll be okay. Just think, someday this could make you very famous. Manager of the world's very first clone, Chuckie. The very first."

"If they're all going to cause this much trouble, I hope he's the last."

Later that night, Wilf sat down and explained his plan to the other Wilf.

"If you can learn the math, language, and science by Saturday," he said at last, "then you can work on social studies all day Sunday. That's my worst subject. I guess I'll have to help you with Life Skills. You can't really learn those things without doing them yourself."

"What things?" asked the other Wilf.

"Sewing stuff and cooking hot dogs."

The other Wilf looked puzzled. "Dogs on fire?"

Slang, Wilf thought. One more little problem. For the first time he started to wonder if maybe he was being crazy as Chuckie had said. But then he shrugged off his fears. The other Wilf had done pretty well already, just listening to WROK. He'd pick things up real fast.

"It's going to be a lot of hard work for you," Wilf told the other Wilf. "But if you really do want to go outside, this is the only way you're going to do it. What do you think?"

"Let's go for the gold," said the other Wilf.

Just before going off to sleep that night, Wilf remembered about French. He couldn't say much more than *parlez-vous français*. Osmosis must not work in foreign languages. And like Life Skills, the other Wilf couldn't just read the book. French words never sounded the way they looked.

He yawned. His brain was tired. Monday was four days away. He was sure an answer would pop up sooner or later. He looked over at the bed. The other Wilf was already curled up and doing that funny little snore/snort. Wilf sighed, then went to the closet to get his sleeping bag.

14

It turned out to be Chuckie who came up with the answer to Wilf's dilemma about French.

On Saturday morning, Wilf, wheeling a grocery cart containing a pound of calves' liver, six Idaho baking potatoes, a head of lettuce, and a bottle of low-calorie salad dressing, turned the corner of the dairy aisle at the Day 'n Night Supermarket and collided with Chuckie, who was browsing through a rack of comic books.

Wilf told Chuckie about how the other Wilf had been studying. "I just gave him my books. He's read most of them already. After everybody went to bed, we sat in the closet with the light on. I asked him some questions from some old tests, and he got most of them all right. He even explained where I'd made my mistakes."

"Don't you think your teachers are going to get suspicious?" asked Chuckie. "It's going to come as a big shock when all of a sudden you start acting intelligent. I mean . . ."

"I told him to begin slow and miss a lot of answers," replied Wilf. "Then he can gradually get better, to make it look like I've started studying. I also showed him where we were in each class. I wouldn't want him to get ahead."

"Good thinking."

"There's only one problem. French." Wilf explained.

Chuckie put the latest issue of *Supernerd* back in the rack. "I think I know how you could do it," he said slowly.

"How?"

"Well, at supper last night, Grams was telling my mom that when she was trying to quit smoking, she used these cassettes that sounded just like regular music. Only there were supposed to be messages on the tape, too. She listened to the tapes with earphones while she was sleeping. She said she couldn't really remember hearing anything, but those messages must have got into her head somehow because she hasn't had a cigarette in seventeen months."

It sounded something like osmosis. "How is that going to help me with French?" Wilf asked, interested.

"They have language tapes at the library, don't they? All you have to do is get a French one, plug him in when he goes to bed — and *voilà!*"

Wilf remembered that word. It meant something like "Presto!"

Chuckie's idea sounded like a good one. At least it was worth a try. Providing he wasn't grounded from the library, he'd go down right now and pick up a tape. He could tell his father he needed to do research for a project. He didn't see how anybody could possibly object to that, although he hoped he wouldn't have to go into much detail.

When he got home, however, he discovered his father had other plans for him. "You'll have plenty of time this afternoon to go to the library," he said. "I want to get some yard work out of the way before it gets any warmer."

While his father started the lawn mower, Wilf plugged in the electric weed whacker and started zapping away at the long grass along the edges of the sidewalk and driveway. The sun was hot on his neck. He found himself thinking about the other Wilf and how great it was going to be to have a clone to take his place at school. Maybe by the year 2015, everyone would have a clone instead of a robot. Then nobody would have to work. It wasn't until he heard his father yell that Wilf realized he'd nearly annihilated a row of brand-new alyssum plants at the edge of the garden.

After the trimming was done, his father asked him to help drag two old mattresses up from the basement to put at the curb for the garbage truck. Wilf looked longingly at the mattresses. Even a broken-down box spring would have felt good. His body was stiff from being scrunched up on the floor all night while the other Wilf slept on his nice soft bed.

A lot of other people on Willowridge seemed to be cleaning out their garages and basements, too. There were boxes and piles of stuff in front of nearly every house. Wilf had just dropped his end of the mattress on the grass strip between the street and sidewalk when he heard the sound of a car engine starting. He glanced up. It looked like the black pickup truck that had been near the Lougens' the other day. It was probably one of those people who drive around looking for broken furniture and things like that to fix up and sell, Wilf thought. He watched, curious, from the edge of the driveway. It had suddenly occurred to him that there must be valuable junk, and then just "junk junk." If he could figure out which was which, maybe he could go into the business himself someday. You didn't have to go to school to be a junk man.

The pickup moved along the street. As it approached his driveway, it slowed. Through the front window, Wilf could see two men in the cab. He was sure they'd be interested in the mattresses, which weren't really dirty or anything, just sagging a bit in the middle. But the

truck didn't stop. It drove right past, and from the passenger side, underneath a thin fringe of dirty brown-gray hair, a pair of strange, pale yellowish eyes focused on Wilf. A cold, clammy feeling washed over him. Quickly, he turned his back to the truck and hurried up the driveway.

Wilf's father was in the kitchen making sandwiches. Everyone else was out. His mother had gone shopping, saying she was sure to be needing new clothes soon, and anyway it would keep her mind off eating. Morticia and her ghoulfriends were in Kathlyn's basement constructing their cauldron out of papier-mâché.

"What on earth has happened to all the peanut butter?" his father complained as he tried to scrape enough from the jar to cover a slice of bread. "I could have sworn there was a full jar just the other day. I can't find that leftover slice of meat loaf, either. Your mother's supposed to be on a diet. I wonder if she's been cheating. She seemed pretty determined, though. And Allana wouldn't dare touch anything that smacked of nutrition, so either I've not only been sleepwalking but also sleep-eating, or else you're going to start looking like a professional wrestler one of these days."

Wilf shrugged, hoping his father would accept that for an answer. It was getting harder and harder to keep the other Wilf's stomach filled. There seemed to be no bottom to it. Besides the piece of cold meat loaf and a bunch of grapes Wilf had manged to sneak up to his room that morning, he had also taken some of his weekly lunch money to the Day 'n Night Supermarket and had bought a half dozen sticks of beef jerky, a bag of potato chips, and three boxes of fruit drink. At the rate the other Wilf was demolishing every morsel that was put in front of him, Wilf figured he'd be broke in less than a week.

Wilf made three baloney and cheese sandwiches, slipping two inside his shirt when his father wasn't looking. After lunch, he excused himself and went up to his room. His father headed for the couch to watch a program on building a deck. Wilf knew it would only be a matter of minutes before he was sound asleep.

"Put the books away for a while," Wilf said after the other Wilf had devoured his sandwiches. "This is important." He pointed at the eight-by-ten photograph of Mrs. Horansky's seventh-grade homeroom that was thumbtacked to the wall over his desk. "These are the kids you're going to be going to school with. You have to know their names so they'll think you're me. I'll point to them. You memorize the faces so you'll know them when you see them, and then repeat their names, okay? Okay. First row. Randall Dorsey."

The other Wilf stared at the picture as if burning it into his brain. "Randall Dorsey," he said.

"Okay, next: Patricia Kline. No, we'd better use nicknames. Patty Kline."

"What's a nickname?"

"It's — well, it's when you shorten a person's real name. Most Patricias are called Patty."

"What's your nickname?"

"Wilf. Actually, it's short for Wilfred, which is sort of short for —"

"You aren't making much sense."

Wilf sighed. "My mother thought I was going to be a boy, see, and she wanted to name me after my father. His name is Allan. But then I was a girl — I mean, my sister came first, so she was Allana. That's more of a girl's name." Wilf doubted if the other Wilf understood the difference between boys and girls, so he hurried on. "My name is a combination of my grandfathers' names: William and Frederick. Understand? Wil-fred."

"What's *my* name?"

"Your name?"

"All these people, the ones you're showing me, they all have names. Aren't I a people?"

"Of course, you are," Wilf began, then stopped. The other Wilf was alive, of course. Whether he was human or not was another question. Real people didn't hatch from OceanPups eggs. On the other hand, if they were going to pull off this scheme of his, Wilf supposed he'd have to have the same name.

He frowned. He'd never been terribly fond of his name, but at least it was his. He didn't know one other kid, or grown-up either, who was called Wilf. Now he would have to share it. And not only his first name, but his last one, too. It didn't seem right, but just then he didn't seem to have any choice in the matter.

"You're going to be me, see, and that means you'll have to have my name. Wilf. That way, when my teachers — I mean, when your teachers — uh, when teachers call on you, they'll really think it's me. The same with the kids at school. They'll call you Wilf because . . ." Wilf gave up. The "you's" and "me's" were getting so confusing, he was never quite sure which of the two of them he was talking about. "Never mind. Just try and get the right names with the right faces. It's important. Now this is Neil Ostereicher."

"Neil Ostereicher."

They finished the first row and started on the second. "Susan —"

"Matthews," said the other Wilf before Wilf even got the word out of his mouth.

"How did you know that?" Wilf asked, puzzled.

The other Wilf shrugged. "It just came to me."

Wilf shook his head. "Next one. Cheryl —"

"Stratton."

Wilf pointed again.

"Garin Shusterman," said the other Wilf. "But sometimes you call him Scuzzy. Is that a nickname?"

Wilf nodded.

The other Wilf then proceeded to correctly identify all seventeen of the remaining kids in the top three rows.

Wilf was so astounded, he forgot being upset about

having to give his name away. He knew there were computers that could identify voices and fingerprints, but he'd never heard of one recognizing a face without ever having seen it before. It was incredible. The plan was going to work. He was sure of it now. Somewhere inside, however, there was still a slight feeling of uneasiness, but he didn't understand what could possibly be wrong.

A little while later, Wilf left for the library. A tall stack of billowy, dark clouds was drifting slowly in the direction of Willowridge Road. Off in the distance he could hear the growl of thunder. He hoped there would be a storm. It wouldn't be quite as exciting as a tornado, but he always liked watching the yellow zigzag bolts of lightning slash across the sky.

The library was very busy. Every chair and table was full. Wilf saw Ellen Anne Vanderhoofft, her nose buried in a book that was about the size of a baby elephant. Still studying. He wondered when she'd ever wake up and discover that there were more interesting things in the world than having a 104 average in math. Wilf tried to imagine a clone of Ellen Anne. Would she have a 208 math average?

Going up to the main desk, Wilf asked the librarian where the language tapes were. She was checking out a huge stack of picture books for a woman with four little kids who were stuck on their mother's legs like they were made out of Velcro. Without missing a beat, she continued to slip cards in each book pocket with one hand and with the other motioned to a rack over near the children's department.

Wilf flipped through the cassettes. He'd never known there were so many different kinds of tapes. There was lots of music, of course, but also old radio shows and even books that you could listen to.

He located the language tapes and pulled out a plastic case that said *Basic French*. When he opened it, however, there was nothing inside. He went back to the desk. The librarian was checking out more books. She told Wilf that the tapes were kept in another place for safety, but that if he wanted to wait, she'd help him as soon as she could.

Wilf stood in line. He could see through a window that the clouds were nearly directly overhead. He hoped he'd have time to get home before the rain began.

At last it was his turn. The librarian took the plastic case, opened a drawer behind the desk, and removed two tapes. She slipped them into the case, then took Wilf's library card and ran it under the electronic scanner.

"These will be due a week from today," she reminded Wilf. She passed him the case and turned her attention to the next customer.

The thunder was growing louder as Wilf left the library. Fortunately, the rain continued to hold off until he was just about to climb the steps to his house. Then the first drops, as big as quarters, plopped onto the sidewalk. Seconds later, the sky was split with a jagged fork of light. The air crackled with energy. A clap of thunder like a thousand pounds of dynamite going off shook the ground under Wilf's feet.

Suddenly, without warning, Wilf felt a scream of terror arise in his throat, and at the same time, there came a terrible urge to run and hide. Somewhere. Anywhere. It didn't matter. All he could think of was that the world was ending.

In panic, Wilf pawed at the screen-door latch. Just as his finger closed on the metal, however, he saw his father stumble sleepily out of the living room and head up the stairs.

"I'm coming, Wilf," he called out. "It's all right. Just thunder."

Wilf dove behind a nearby juniper bush. A torrent of rain poured off the eaves and soaked him through to his skin. He wiped his face and took several deep breaths. Slowly he began to calm down and could think straight again.

The scream, he was pretty sure, hadn't come from him, but from inside the house. It must have been the other Wilf. Of course. A thunderstorm would frighten anyone who hadn't experienced one before. But why had he, Wilf, felt the terror, too? He'd been through hundreds of storms. It was — well, almost as if the other Wilf had somehow transmitted his own fear to Wilf. Was that possible?

Confused, miserable, and wet, Wilf crouched in the bushes and waited. By now his father was finding out that the Wilf in the bedroom wasn't his son. Wilf had been crazy to think that he could hide a thing like a clone for very long. Besides, he didn't exactly feel very comfortable keeping a secret from his parents. Sooner or later he was going to have to explain what was going on. He might as well go up there right now and get it over with.

But just as he was about to leave the shelter of the juniper, he heard his father, warbling something about "pennies from heaven," come strolling down the stairs and fade off in the direction of the kitchen. He didn't sound very excited. Could it be . . . ? Cautiously, Wilf stood up and peered through the screen. His father was still singing. So, trailing a small river of water behind him, Wilf scurried up the stairs and into his bedroom.

"You're wet," the other Wilf greeted him. "Did you hear that noise? Man, I thought it was the end of the world! But then my father came and sat on the bed for a while. I pretended I was asleep. I didn't want him to dissect me."

Well, maybe, thought Wilf, his decision to confess going out the window, maybe it wouldn't hurt to wait. Just a little while longer.

15

From behind the curtains of the living room, Wilf watched anxiously for the first sight of Chuckie and the other Wilf. It was nearly half past three. What could be keeping them?

The other Wilf had gone downstairs at precisely 7:40 that morning. Wilf had calculated it to the minute, leaving just enough time for him to toss down a glass of juice, grab his lunch bag, and say "I'm late," before flying out the door to meet Chuckie. Wilf had watched him go down the sidewalk, looking around with wonder at his first glimpse of the world outside. He bent down and ran his hand over the grass, then made a brief detour over to the ring of bright pansies that grew around the base of the dogwood tree. Fortunately, before he could waste any more time, Chuckie came down the street and took him by the arm, and the two of them went off together.

The rest of the family had followed a short time later, leaving Wilf alone.

He'd spent half the day chewing on his knuckles and listening to all the little sounds that he'd never known a house could make. Just the refrigerator starting up made him jump. A couple of times, a breeze had caught the front screen door and banged it, sending Wilf scurrying to safety under the bed. Once or twice, the phone rang. He didn't answer it.

He wondered why he was so on edge. After all, he'd gone over every single instruction with the other Wilf six times.

"Now, the shorter length of time you stay in any one situation," he'd explained the night before, "the less chance there'll be of anyone suspecting you're not the real me." Every time he said something like that, he had a creepy feeling that somehow the other Wilf *was* the real him, only it didn't really make any sense, so he tried to forget about it as much as possible. "Don't get into any long conversations, either. At least not at first. 'Hi' and 'See ya' will do fine for a while, except in class. If a teacher asks a question, stutter a little bit and then answer it. It probably would help," he added, "if you look sort of surprised that you did it."

Yes, he was satisfied that he'd done the best he could. The other Wilf would be able to manage on his own. He, Wilf, would have to stop worrying.

Oddly enough, what kept creeping into his thoughts, although he desperately tried to keep it out, was school. He could almost hear the squeak of the chalk as Ellen Anne Vanderhoofft, the math wizard, wove a mile-long equation across three sections of blackboard. He wondered who was in the nurse's office with what ailment. He also, briefly, very briefly, had a strange, almost friendly, vision of Heather Spears-Croxton.

Wilf had read a story once by H. G. Wells, called *The Invisible Man*. He'd thought it would be fun being invisible. Right now he could be wandering around the halls of Gatesburg East Junior High without having to show up for a single class. If scientists had figured out a way to make clones, someday they could probably mix up a concoction to turn people into ghosts. But not the dead kind. Sort of like spirits. Wilf already knew how to send invisible messages by dipping a toothpick into lemon juice and using it like a pen. You couldn't see any writing, but when the person who got the message held it over a hot light bulb, yellowish-brown words showed up. He didn't suppose pouring a bottle of lemon juice over himself would work, but it was interesting to think about.

Now the hands of the little gold clock that stood over the fireplace had inched along until it was almost four o'clock. School had been out for over an hour. Wilf was worried. What if something had happened to the other Wilf? What if he caught the flu and had to go to the nurse's office? What if the nurse had called his parents to come for him? This time he wouldn't be so lucky.

His insides were just about to knit themselves into an afghan when Chuckie and the other Wilf appeared at the corner, walking and chatting the same way he and Chuckie had been doing for years. Watching them together gave Wilf an odd feeling, almost like he *was* invisible.

"What kept you so long?" Wilf demanded when they were inside.

"I had to write," said the other Wilf, and then announced, "I need food." He headed off in the direction of the kitchen.

"Write?" Wilf looked at Chuckie.

"Detention," explained Chuckie.

"The first time he's even in a school and he gets detention? For what?"

"Acting up in French class. I had to wait for him. I was afraid he'd get lost on the way home."

Wilf groaned. The other Wilf had worn the headphones to bed both Saturday and Sunday nights. Because there were also important things like teaching him how to write, Wilf hadn't had time to check on whether Chuckie's idea had worked. He'd just hoped that Mrs. Mounce, Sr., had been right when she said she'd picked up messages in her sleep. At the worst, he'd figured that if Miss Beausoleil had asked the other Wilf to say anything, he'd just look dumb, the same way the real Wilf usually did.

The other Wilf came back, munching on what looked like a fourteen-year-old chunk of salami.

"What did you do in French class that you got detention?" Wilf asked him.

"Nuh-" The other Wilf swallowed. "Nothing. The teacher asked me a question and I answered it."

"What did she ask you?"

"How I would say, 'Good morning, my friend.' "

"And?"

"And?"

"And you said . . ."

"I said, 'Доброе утро, мой друг.' "

Wilf gaped at the other Wilf. *What?*

"Доброе утро, мой друг," repeated the other Wilf. "It means, 'Good morning, my friend.' Then, if you're at the market, you can ask, 'У вао еств сегодня свежие курицы?' That's 'Do you have any fresh chickens today?' "

It suddenly occurred to Wilf that he might be wrong about the other Wilf not being from outer space. Listening to the strange language, he was now certain that aliens from the planet Zorgon had indeed invaded Earth. They'd zeroed in on the Farkuses because they were a normal Earth family. Eventually they'd send other clones in other OceanPups eggs to impersonate his father and his mother. Maybe even Morticia, if they could figure her out. Then they'd send the real Farkuses to Zorgon as slaves. After that, the Zorgonians could take over the entire city of Gatesburg.

Wilf began to walk backward, keeping his arms out in front of his face as protection. "Get away from me. That isn't French," he said to the other Wilf. His teeth were chattering. "It's — it's *Zorgonese*. If you take one more step, I'm calling the Army!"

The other Wilf took three more steps forward. "Нет," he said.

"Wilf, wait!" yelled Chuckie as Wilf reached for the phone, which wasn't in its cradle anyway. Wilf froze. "You're right. He's not talking French. I heard Gorbachev say that word the other night on the news. 'Net' means 'No.' He's speaking Russian!"

16

Up in his bedroom, Wilf looked in dismay at the title on the tape he'd just removed from the Walkman. *Russian for Beginners*. He couldn't believe it. The librarian must have gotten the cassettes mixed up. He hadn't even thought to check.

"I'm a genius!" crowed Chuckie. "An absolute genius! Didn't I tell you? Wow! It's like mind control!"

"Как мы выбираемся из этого затора уличого движения?" said the other Wilf.

"What the heck does that mean?" asked Wilf.

"How do we get out of this traffic jam?"

Wilf sighed. "Well," he said, "I guess I could go back to the library for the French tapes and try it again." He sat down on the bed and began to pull on his sneakers. The librarian had better pay more attention this time, though, or the other Wilf would be walking around like a one-man United Nations.

"I have to take a quiz," announced the other Wilf. He started out the door.

"That's *whiz*," corrected Chuckie, laughing. "I have to go, too. Leave, I mean. I'm supposed to be playing video games with Scuzzy Shusterman at Blinky's Deli."

"Can I play video games, too?" asked the other Wilf.

"No," snapped Wilf. For some reason, he felt irritable. "You know we can't both be outside at the same time, even if we weren't grounded."

"Yeah. If they ever found out about you, you'd be a goner." Chuckie zipped his forefinger down his chest like he was slicing it open. Then his eyes shifted from one Wilf to the other. "Of course, they might not know which you was which."

"They're not going to get a chance to find out, either," declared Wilf. "We made a deal. He gets to go to school, that's all. I do everything else."

"You don't know anything about video games, anyway," Chuckie pointed out to the other Wilf. "Maybe in a few weeks, if you can stay out of detention, we'll go to Blinky's on the way home and I'll show you how they work."

Chuckie and Wilf walked out of the bedroom together. Sure, and don't forget to show him how to play Depth Rescue, Wilf muttered silently to Chuckie's back. He'll be the new champion in three minutes. Wilf had

had the all-time highest score the week before he was grounded. Using only one submersible, he'd worked his way down from the surface ship, past the sharks and barracuda, wrestled all six octopi at a thousand points each, and escaped from the sea serpent (5,000 points). He'd even gotten within sight of the sunken schooner when an eel had slipped out from a rock and electrocuted him. The other Wilf would, Wilf was positive, easily swim into the schooner, recover the chest full of gold bullion, and get his name posted permanently on the video machine. Of course, it would be Wilf's name, too, but he'd know it wasn't him who had earned it.

Grumpily, Wilf jammed his foot in one sneaker and yanked on the laces. One of them snapped off in his hand. He threw the broken piece of lace on the floor in disgust, then tied knots at the ends of the two ends in his sneaker. Lots of kids wore their shoes loose like that. He fixed the other lace the same way and started out of the room. His head was just clearing the door frame when he saw a flash of black at the top of the stairs. Quickly he ducked back in the room, dropped to the floor, and wriggled under the bed.

"Well, if it isn't Mr. Personality himself," Wilf heard Morticia say. "I met Marilee Manzetti and some of her friends on the way home from rehearsal, and all they could talk about was how cute Wilf Farkus had been in the cafeteria today."

"C-cute?" Chuckie's voice sounded shaky.

"Something about him doing a dance with a piece of pizza."

"Pizza!" yelped the other Wilf. "Do you have some? I love it! It's wonderful. It's — it's молодец!"

Wilf covered his face with his hands. Outside in the hall, there was silence. Then Wilf heard a strange sound. Morticia was giggling!

"Where'd you learn how to do *that*?" she said. "Show me the steps." Wilf heard feet shuffling on the carpet, then a couple of soft thuds. "Cool!" Morticia exclaimed. "Kathlyn and I might be able to work this into our witch scene." She laughed. "You know, I'm actually beginning to think there's hope for you yet, Wilf. Mom and Dad couldn't possibly have raised a complete dud."

The shuffling noise continued on down the hall, accompanied by a cheerful humming. Wilf's body went limp. Morticia, who normally had something critical to say about everything he said or did, had for some reason completely overlooked the fact that her brother, or the person she assumed was her brother, was suddenly speaking Russian. In fact, she was being almost pleasant, which was even more peculiar. While he waited for the other Wilf to come back from the bathroom, Wilf wondered about Morticia.

17

Wilf passed the bowl of mixed vegetables to his father without taking any for himself. A few minutes later, a steaming spoonful of peas, carrots, corn, and beans was slipped onto his plate.

"Eat your vitamins," his mother said, returning the empty spoon to the bowl. "You'll be spurting up pretty soon and you'll need them. Strong bones and muscles don't grow on trees."

Only in OceanPups kits, Wilf thought.

"How are those grades coming along?" asked his father. "Exams must be right around the corner. You've been spending a lot of time on that science project. I hope you're not letting your other subjects slide."

"Don't pressure him so much," Wilf's mother said. "He's had a rough enough time being grounded for almost two months. I'm sure Wilf wants to do a good job, just as much as you want him to."

"I am not pressuring him, Rosemary. I merely asked about school. Can't I express a little interest in my son without people thinking I'm some kind of an ogre? I want the boy to have a good education so he won't end up bagging groceries at the Day 'n Night Supermarket."

"You won't have to worry about him, Dad," Morticia piped up. "From what I saw today, he's got a great future on the stage."

"Stage?" His father glanced at him sharply. "I thought you were starting to get your act together — no pun intended. Or has your sister gotten you involved in this weird Shakespearean production, too?"

"N-n-no," stammered Wilf.

"Then what does she mean?"

"Uh, I — I —" Wilf floundered. He had no idea, except that it had something to do with the other Wilf, pizza, and dancing. Maybe the other Wilf had been out in the sun too long and had developed a bad case of phototaxis. "I was just having a little fun for a change," he said miserably.

"Come on, Wilf," Morticia begged. "Show Mom and Dad the dance you taught me in the hall this afternoon. We can do it together. Watch, you guys. It's really funky." She got up and hopped on one foot while her other leg wiggled around in the air making strange contortions. "Come *on,* Wilf!"

Wilf stayed planted in his seat. He picked up his fork, speared a green bean, and stuck it in his mouth. He was aware that his father was watching him. Finally, he stopped chewing. "I'm not goofing off, Dad. And I'm doing a lot better in school. Honest. In fact, I could possibly get a B or two on my finals."

His father's eyes widened. "B's? Allana, sit down and

stop rattling the dishes!" He turned back to Wilf. "What did you do, find a genie in a bottle?"

"Al!"

It was on the tip of Wilf's tongue to tell his father that although that hadn't exactly been the case, it was pretty close. But he couldn't very well do that, so he gave a weak grin and went back to his vegetables.

"And speaking of Shakespeare," asked Wilf's mother, changing the subject to Wilf's intense relief, "when are we going to get a chance to see Macbeth à la New Wave?"

Morticia gave a practiced cackle that sent shivers up and down Wilf's spine. "Two weeks from Saturday. There's a dress rehearsal the night before." The phone rang. "I'll get it," she said, jumping up again. "It's probably Kathlyn."

"What a surprise," observed Wilf's father dryly.

Morticia came back into the dining room carrying the phone and wearing a big smirk. "It's for you," she told Wilf, and probably everyone within the city limits of Gatesburg. "It's a *g-i-r-l*."

The back of Wilf's neck felt like someone had aimed a hair dryer at it. "I'll take it in the kitchen," he heard himself croak.

"I thought the use of the telephone was included in his grounding," his father said as Wilf rose.

"It's a girl," his mother said. "Didn't you hear?"

"So?"

Morticia and his mother exchanged smiles. Wilf escaped with the phone.

"Hello?" he said, as soon as he was far enough away so the rest of the family couldn't hear.

"Hi, Wilf."

Wilf didn't recognize the voice, but the girl on the other end of the receiver seemed to assume he knew who she was, so he pretended he did. "Hi."

"I had a dentist appointment today. I hear I missed your great footwork in the cafeteria. Everybody said it was really spectacular. They're calling it the Farkus Funk."

Wilf wished he'd really been the Invisible Man. It would help if he understood just what had gone on in school that day. In just a few hours, it seemed, the other Wilf had made sure that he'd never feel like a wildebeest again. Now everyone knew Wilf Farkus, except that they didn't really know which Wilf Farkus they knew. Wilf felt himself getting confused again.

"Who is this?" he asked, getting back to the beginning of the conversation.

She didn't answer right away, and when she did, there was a sort of edge to her voice. "It's Heather, of course. I was supposed to call you tonight, or do you have so many girlfriends, you can't remember?"

Great. This was just what he needed. As if it wasn't bad enough that he was famous for inventing a dance he'd never even seen, now here he was, stuck in still another mess. One that apparently involved his having a girlfriend.

"Uh, I just took a shower," he said, thinking furiously. "I got water in my ears."

"Oh. Well, that's all right, then," Heather said.

Wilf waited another long minute for her to continue. When she didn't, he said, "Okay, see you tomorrow," and got ready to hang up.

"Wait a minute. What about the corsage?"

"Corsage?"

"For the dance. I had to ask my mother what she thought would go with my yellow dress. She suggested daisies."

It was his own fault, Wilf thought miserably. He didn't want to go to any silly old dance. He should have told her that when Marilee Manzetti had first mentioned it. The trouble was, he didn't think Heather was the type who'd take no for an answer.

Then, in a flash, he remembered something and knew how he could get out of at least one of his problems. The best part was that he wouldn't have to lie, or even tell a half-lie like the *Weekly Screamer*.

"I feel real bad about this, Heather," he said. He tried to sound disappointed, but it was hard. "My parents grounded me for the rest of the school year because of my grades. I can't go to the dance. In fact, I can't go anywhere. Maybe some other time." Or some other century, he added silently.

The slamming on the other end of the line hurt his ear. He'd have to warn the other Wilf that school might be hard on him for the next few days. It probably wouldn't matter to him, though. It wasn't as if he had feelings.

Wilf went back to the dining room. His mother was talking about the new building in downtown Gatesburg. It had an open-air courtyard in the center that was really a greenhouse and florist shop. His mother was a salesperson for Spaces, Inc., which rented offices to companies. She liked her job. Wilf sometimes wondered what would happen if she really did win the *Reader's Digest* Sweepstakes. She'd probably still work but might possibly trade her old Chevette in for a Porsche.

"Was that Heather?" asked Morticia, whose mouth was just finishing a yawn.

"Heather who?" asked his mother.

"And Heather why?" asked his father.

"Wilf's going to the seventh-grade dance," Morticia put in. "He's taking Heather Spears-Croxton."

"Gloria's daughter? Gloria Spears was a friend of your Aunt Julia, I think," his mother said. "At least, they were active in some of the same causes."

"Another one of the braless wonders?" asked Wilf's father, smirking. "And since when are they having dances in seventh grade? I never got mixed up with girls until I was at least eighteen. That's one problem a boy Wilf's age doesn't need."

Wilf agreed with that.

"Times change," his mother said. "Twelve-year-olds are pretty sophisticated these days. In case you haven't noticed, they don't shoot marbles or play cops and robbers anymore." Turning to Wilf, she said, "I suppose you'll need some new clothes. Those T-shirts and jeans you've been wearing constantly really have to go. A navy-blue blazer would be nice. And some gray slacks."

"*Mother!*" groaned Morticia. "Kids don't dress like corporate executives. Wilf has an image to maintain. A nice shirt and a pair of those baggy slacks with all the pockets and flaps would be just perfect. In black, of course."

"I don't need any clothes," Wilf interrupted. "I told Heather I couldn't go because I'm grounded." He had another sudden inspiration. "Anyway, Dad's right. Exams start the week after the dance. I'll need time to study if I'm going to get those B's."

"Nonsense," his mother said. "You can't just cram everything in at the last minute. You need to take a break once in a while. And I don't want you disappointing that girl. You go right in there and call her back."

Wilf waited for his father to object and say that his mother was coddling him again. Instead, his father sighed, pushed his chair back from the table, and got up. "Far be it from me to second-guess two such outstanding authorities on fashion and matters of the heart.

Just don't ask me to teach him the gavotte. I'm definitely out of practice."

"Oh, don't be a spoilsport," said his mother. "What happened to the romance in your soul?"

"I left it with my heart in San Francisco."

18

Under his mother's watchful eye, and with Morticia smirking in the background, Wilf called Heather and told her that his parents had changed their minds and that he'd be happy to take her to the dance. It wasn't even a *Weekly Screamer*–type lie. It was what his father would have called a whopper.

Heather accepted the news without comment, except to repeat that her corsage had to be daisies. "I also think it would be nice if we sat at the same lunch table from now on," she added.

Wilf struggled to find the words to tell her what he thought of that idea, then, seeing his mother still watching him, gave up. "Sure," he said. After all, what did it matter to him if the whole school thought he and Heather were madly in love? It would be the other Wilf who would have to take all the jokes and ridicule. He, Wilf, wasn't even going to be involved.

He realized he'd made a mistake by neglecting to tell the other Wilf about Heather and the whole business with the dance. There'd been so many things to think about and remember, it had completely slipped his mind.

Of course, he, the real Wilf, would be the one to go to the dance. There was no doubt about that. His mother would be fussing over every little detail right up until the last minute, as mothers usually did — making sure his shirt was tucked in and that he'd brushed his teeth and stuff like that. It would be much too risky to let the other Wilf take his place. They'd been able to fool Morticia a couple of times, and his father the day of the thunderstorm, but his mother was something else. Mothers knew their kids.

But the dance would last only a couple of hours. Wilf thought he could survive for that long. It would be one of those times his father was always talking about when he said, "Once in a while you'll find you have to do something you don't like. Do it anyway. You'll come out a winner in the end." Wilf wondered what his father would say if he knew the "prize" was going to be Heather Spears-Croxton.

"Okay, I want to hear exactly what went on today," Wilf told the other Wilf later that night after the house quieted down.

The other Wilf was in his usual place in the closet,

sitting on a sort of nest he'd made out of baseball mitts, street-hockey shin guards, and some sweatpants that Wilf had outgrown. If anyone looked in there, however, it wouldn't seem like anything other than Wilf's usual pile of junk.

The other Wilf didn't immediately answer Wilf's question about school. He seemed to be absorbed in Wilf's science book, *This Great Planet Earth*. The book was opened to a picture of the human circulation system. It reminded Wilf of a road map, with all the blue and red lines running over the outline of a body.

"What's this?" the other Wilf asked, pointing.

Wilf peered down. "A heart. Everybody has one."

"Me, too?"

Wilf wasn't quite sure, but he figured since the outside of the other Wilf looked exactly like him, the inside probably did, too, so he said yes.

"What does my chart do?"

"Heart," said Wilf. "Your heart is like a pump. It keeps the blood moving around to your arms and legs and head and —"

The other Wilf held his hand up in front of his face. "There's blood in there?" he asked.

Wilf nodded.

"And some of it's red and some blue."

"No. It's all red."

"Then why —?"

Wilf's osmosis deserted him. "Never mind about

that," he said quickly, so the other Wilf wouldn't find out that he didn't know the answer, either. "I have to talk to you about Heather Spears-Croxton."

The other Wilf frowned. "Heather? Oh, yeah. Now I remember. She's the girl who needs a corset."

"Corsage," corrected Wilf.

"She said something about a dance. Is that like this?" The other Wilf bounded to his feet and started the crazy jumping routine that Wilf had seen Morticia do at dinner.

"Shhh!" hissed Wilf. "Somebody's going to hear you."

The other Wilf sank down in his nest again.

Wilf sighed.

"I like Heather," the other Wilf said suddenly. "She's one sharp cookie."

"And the moon is made of green cheese," muttered Wilf.

"Really?"

"No."

The other Wilf looked puzzled, then apparently decided he wasn't going to understand Wilf's comment even if he explained it. "She's not as silly as the other girls at school." He reached out and clutched Wilf's ankle. "Oh, Wilf, you have such beautiful eyes," he said in a high-pitched voice. "You look like a movie star. And I just love your curly brown hair."

"Cut it out, will you?" Wilf pulled his leg free and

cast a worried look toward his bedroom door. "Look, from now on, Heather wants you to sit with her in the cafeteria at lunchtime. Come to think of it, it's not a bad idea. Then after school, you can tell me everything she said."

"Why?"

"Because I have to go to this dance with her. Naturally she's going to mention what went on in school. I'd come off pretty stupid if I didn't know what she was talking about. Understand?"

"Okay. But why can't I go to the dance?"

"Because you can't." He tried to explain about mothers — even mother animals — and how they had an almost unexplainable way of recognizing their young. The other Wilf listened politely, but Wilf could tell he wasn't getting through.

"And what about Sunday?" the other Wilf said after Wilf gave up and stopped talking.

"Sunday?"

"I'm supposed to take Heather to a movie. She told me."

Wilf groaned. A tornado couldn't possibly create more havoc than Heather Spears-Croxton was stirring up. "You're going to have to tell Heather that I'm — uh, you're — busy studying for final exams. Say that if I — you don't pass everything, uh, you might have to go to a private school next year."

"Will I?"

114 •

"Not if you play your cards right."

"Like solitaire?"

"No. It's just an expression. But if you — uh, I — get good grades, I'll be able to stay at Gatesburg East."

"Where will I go?"

That question had been slipping, unwelcome, into Wilf's head for some time, especially when he was trying hard to keep from thinking about it. He'd known all along that he wouldn't be able to keep the other Wilf hidden forever. So far he'd gotten away with his brilliant plan. All he had to do now was make it through exams. After that, he guessed Chuckie's idea about the shopping mall was as good as any. He couldn't just send the other Wilf back to The Impossibility Company like a lamp he'd ordered from a catalog and then decided he didn't want after all. Although he'd certainly thought about it. He'd read the Life Insurance Policy that had come with the OceanPups kit, too. It was only good if the OceanPups died, and then they would just replace them with more OceanPups. Suppose the same thing happened — only worse? Suppose he got Dracula?

Yes, the mall would be best. Somebody would be sure to find him wandering around all by himself and take him to the police station. He wouldn't have any identification. The police would think he was an orphan and put him in an orphanage. Then he, the real Wilf, would have the whole summer to get ready for a fresh start in eighth grade. But not in a private school.

Wilf shoved the problem to the back of his mind again. "We'll cross that bridge when we come to it. Later," he translated.

"Okay."

Wilf went on. "Now, what about this big deal about pizza? You were supposed to stay in the background, not make yourself the talk of the whole school."

The other Wilf cocked his head. "Don't you want people to like you?"

"Sure, I want them to like me."

"Then why are you so grumpy?"

"I'm not grumpy. I'm just worried about what would happen to you if anybody found out you're not me."

"Why do I keep getting the feeling that's not the whole truth?"

Wilf's thoughts instantly returned to the Zorgonians. It was pretty weird the way the other Wilf kept tuning in to his brain waves.

"Anyway," the other Wilf went on when Wilf didn't answer, "about the pizza. I guess I got carried away. It's just that I've never tasted anything so — so —"

"Молодец!" said Wilf wearily. He supposed that meant something like "awesome." In Russian.

19

The other Wilf quickly settled into a routine. Every morning he went downstairs at the last minute, grabbed a bowl of cereal, and rushed out before anybody could start up a conversation. From the upstairs window, Wilf would watch him meet Chuckie and set off toward school. And every time, for just a minute, he had an odd feeling that he was still somehow in the middle of a bad dream. Or a comic book.

At first, Wilf enjoyed having time to himself. He reread the *Lord of the Rings* trilogy, although not as fast as the other Wilf had. He listened to WROK with his headset on and doodled cartoon characters on the backs of his old homework papers. The ones with the D's and F's. The only schoolwork he did was to stick some labels on the bones of his old cardboard Halloween skeleton and have the other Wilf hand it in to Mrs. Donnally for his science project. He still wondered if his OceanPups would have gotten an A if they'd turned out the way they were supposed to.

After school, the two changed places. The other Wilf stayed in the bedroom, and the real Wilf was the one who ran errands to the Day 'n Night Supermarket, sat with the family at dinner, and usually ended up having to do the dishes.

Partway through the second week of this, however, Wilf found himself thinking more and more about summer and how glad he'd be when it finally came. A person could only watch so many game shows. He was also getting tired of digging around in the refrigerator to find something to eat that his mother wouldn't miss. He itched to be outside, stretching his legs with a good game of soccer or Capture the Flag with Chuckie and Shusterman and some of the other guys. He was to the point where he was almost looking forward to being pushed around a dance floor for three hours by Heather Spears-Croxton at the seventh-grade dance. But not quite.

Last Tuesday, his mother had taken him and Morticia to the Covington Shopping Centre. They spent an hour and a half going in and out of most of the ninety-seven stores. It had only taken fifteen minutes to pick out pants and a shirt for him. The rest of the time was devoted to Morticia's search for the perfect pair of shoes. When she did her dance around the cauldron, she said, everyone would notice them.

"Especially Todd," she observed as she finally stood before the floor mirror in Fielding's and admired her feet, which were encased in a pair of black flats that were, to Wilf's eyes, exactly like the pair she'd just taken off. She practiced a few jumps of the other Wilf's dance just to make sure they wouldn't fall off on stage.

"Todd?" asked Wilf's mother.

Aha, thought Wilf. No wonder Morticia had been a little preoccupied lately.

Morticia's eyes glazed over. "Todd Carmichael. He has the lead. He's a wonderful Macbeth. Everyone says so. He's going to study acting in college. He has his own car, too," she finished dreamily.

"I hope you weren't planning to ride in it," Wilf's mother said.

Morticia came back to earth with a thud. "He *asked* me, Mom!"

"Then have him *un*ask you. Allana, neither your father nor I feel you're quite old enough for cars just yet."

"But he wants to take me to the Snack Palace after rehearsal on Friday. I already said I'd go. I'll absolutely die of embarrassment if I have to tell him I can't! He'll think I'm a *child!*"

"I'm sorry, Allana, but this is not a negotiable point. Do you still want the shoes?" Wilf's mother unzipped one of the compartments in her purse and took out a credit card.

Morticia's lower lip started to stick out in one of her classic pouts, but then she thought better of it, removed the shoes, carefully set them in the box, said, "Yes, please," and held out her hand.

Finally, for Wilf, the end appeared to be in sight. It was Thursday. Tomorrow was the dance, with exams scheduled to start the next Monday. For some reason, Wilf had woken up more on edge than usual. As soon as the other Wilf went downstairs, he took up his usual post at the window. A soft, warm wind gently nudged the curtains. As Wilf stood there fighting down an urge to pace, Chuckie came around the corner. He was swinging his knapsack and doing a little step that Wilf recognized as part of the Farkus Funk. The front door opened, and the other Wilf appeared halfway down the walk.

Then . . .

"Wilf!"

Wilf became a statue. Chuckie's knapsack did one last loop, then dropped and hung limp. Wilf's mother was striding toward the other Wilf, a piece of paper in her outstretched hand. She said something to him. He nodded, took the paper, and stuffed it in his pocket. Nervously, Wilf waited for her to go back in the house. But she didn't. She stayed there talking. And laughing. And talking some more. The other Wilf was talking and laughing, too. Then, suddenly, his mother planted a kiss on the other Wilf's cheek, gave him a hug, and disappeared from Wilf's view.

Wilf stumbled back from the window, his hand to his face. He'd felt his mother's kiss as if he himself had been on the sidewalk! He didn't understand why, but that wasn't what had given him the biggest shock. His mother hadn't known it was him! She'd been that close and still thought the other Wilf was her own son!

Silently, he crept back into his sleeping bag under the bed and huddled there, terrified. What was happening? His own mother! And he'd been worried that his plan to use the other Wilf as a substitute might not work! Well, it had worked beyond his wildest imagination. In fact, it couldn't have been worse if the other Wilf really *was* an alien and had taken over his body! It was almost the same. He was taking over Wilf's life! But which of their lives was the real one? He almost didn't know anymore.

But his mother should have! She should have recognized him instantly. No, wait! What if . . . ?

Wilf didn't want to even admit this, but the idea had been persistently growing: what if she *did* know? Or at least suspected? And what if she liked the other Wilf better? After all, he looked the same and talked the same. Except *he* probably took out the garbage without being reminded and carried his empty cereal bowl to the sink. As far as his father was concerned, the other Wilf would suit him just fine, too. There'd be no D's, or even any hooks, on *his* report card.

As soon as the house was quiet, Wilf went in search of the phone. He would call The Impossibility Company. Now. Before things got any worse. He'd tell the men that he wasn't interested in any insurance policy. He didn't want a refund, or an exchange, either. He only wanted them to come and collect their mistake. His OceanPups were defective. Oh, boy, were they ever! But, he decided, he wouldn't mention anything about clones. He'd let them find out on their own, just as he had. Then after they all left, he would just go on as if nothing had ever happened. So what if he'd have to take a couple of dumb exams? It wouldn't be the end of the world. Maybe, if he was lucky and his osmosis was working, he might even do well enough to pass. But even if he failed and had to go to a private school, it would be worth it. At least he'd still have his own life. Not to mention his own parents!

The antenna to the portable phone was sticking out from behind the toaster on the kitchen counter. Wilf began to press the buttons of the hotline number. He knew the number by heart: 1-800-555-PUPS. It rang twice. Then some metal-sounding bleeps came over the receiver and a hollow female computer-voice said in Wilf's ear,

"I'm sorry, but the number you have reached, 1-800-555-7877, has been disconnected. Please check your directory or ask an operator for assistance. Thank you."

"School was great!" cried the other Wilf the minute he and Chuckie got in the door later that afternoon. "We pigged out all day. Miss Beausoleil had things called croissants, and Craig Chu brought in a bag of Chinese fortune cookies. Mine said, 'When in trouble, sometimes it is wiser to use feet than brains.' "

"They made him do the Farkus Funk in social studies," Chuckie told Wilf. "He said Mr. Oldak laughed."

Mr. Oldak had never had a sense of humor where *he* was concerned, Wilf grumbled silently to himself.

"And Mrs. Anselm, my guidance counselor, stopped me in the hall and said she was delighted with the improvement in my attitude. She said she planned to call my parents and tell them —"

"*My* parents," said Wilf, irritated.

The other Wilf didn't stop. "— that I'll probably pass all my subjects and that they won't need to think about sending me to a private school." He beamed. "I did good, didn't I?"

"You sure did," said Chuckie. "Didn't he, Wilf?"

Wilf didn't answer.

"Some kids were putting up colored paper strings all over the cafeteria," the other Wilf continued. "It's for the dance. And great big round squishy things."

"Balloons," said Chuckie. "Listen to this, Wilf. He thought they were something to eat and tried to bite one!"

"BANG!" yelled the other Wilf. "Wow! I thought my nose was history!" He clutched his chest, staggered around, then dropped to the floor and was still.

A giggle escaped from Chuckie's mouth. "Man, he

sure is fun, Wilf," he whispered. "I wish we could keep him."

"Well, we can't," Wilf whispered back. Chuckie was sounding as if the other Wilf was a stray dog or something.

The other Wilf rose, kicked off his Athletix sneakers, and slipped the earphones to the Walkman over his head, twirling the dial to find WROK.

Chuckie watched him. "Well, it's too bad he can't at least go to the dance. Everybody's going to be expecting him to do his thing, and you don't even want to learn it."

"So I'll be the class dud — is that what you're trying to say?"

Chuckie hesitated. "Not really," he said slowly. "It's just that . . ."

Wilf knew he was stuck. The Impossibility Company had moved, or closed, or gone bankrupt, or something. He'd spent the rest of the day trying to think of what he should do. After tying his brain nearly in knots, he'd decided that if he couldn't send the other Wilf back, he might as well go through with his plan. Maybe he'd overreacted again. His mother had probably had some big office rental on her mind that morning and hadn't really been paying much attention.

"I'd gladly stay home," Wilf said, annoyed because that was exactly what he was: the class dud. It was the other Wilf that everyone wanted at the dance. "But you saw what happened with my mother this morning. That was too close a call."

"Well . . ."

Wilf looked at the other Wilf, who had taken off the earphones and was listening in on the conversation. "You two have it all worked out, don't you?"

"It was his idea," said Chuckie defensively.

"It'll be duck soup, Wilf," said the other Wilf. "You get dressed, just like you planned, and let our mother fuss all she wants. You leave the house, on your way to pick up Heather — only when you get around the corner, you cut back through the yards and go in the garage."

"What am I going to do in there?"

"Change clothes with Wilf," said Chuckie.

"I *am* Wilf," Wilf reminded him.

"The other Wilf, then," Chuckie said.

"I could sneak out while everybody's paying attention to you," the other Wilf went on. "We switch clothes. I go get Heather. You stay in the garage until our parents go out."

Wilf hesitated, unable to completely shake off his feelings from earlier in the day. Then he thought about Heather Spears-Croxton. The fact that the other Wilf was actually attracted to her made Wilf more and more positive that he couldn't possibly be human.

"Be my guest," he said.

20

"Straighten up, Wilf! How do you expect your clothes to hang properly when your spine is like a glob of Silly Putty?"

Wilf sighed and shifted his weight from his left foot to his right. He wished his mother would stop twitching his collar and tugging on his shirt sleeves. He wasn't going to be in his clothes long enough for anybody to see them.

"There," she said, picking an invisible speck of lint from Wilf's shoulder. "Doesn't he look terrific?"

Wilf's father put down his newspaper. "Very nice. But then, all Farkus men are handsome, so what's the big deal?"

"In the words of your daughter, spare me," laughed Wilf's mother. "And speaking of handsome men, aren't you going to get dressed? You have a major date yourself tonight, remember?"

"Yeah." His father winked at Wilf. "With this skinny chick. Five pounds she's lost already. I hope there aren't any single guys at this restaurant we're going to. I'll have to beat them off with a stick."

"Thanks for the compliment, dear, but you won't have to worry. I may go absolutely bonkers at the sight of something that doesn't resemble rabbit food and put those five pounds right back."

"The bigger the figure, the more I can love," warbled Wilf's father, dodging a kick that was aimed at his ankle.

"I have to go now, Mom," Wilf said, edging toward the front hall. "I'm supposed to pick Heather up at a quarter to eight."

Morticia came bounding down the stairs, ready for her dress rehearsal. She hit the floor at the bottom, threw her hands into the air, and uttered an ear-piercing shriek. Wilf's father, who had been in the process of folding up the newspaper, suddenly found himself holding two halves of the editorial page.

Morticia was an eerie sight. She was wearing a pair of shiny, skintight black pants that ended just below her knees. Over the top, she had on a long-sleeved black T-shirt with *Shakespeare* written down the left sleeve in big white letters. Her face had been tinted a sickly green color, and her eyes were outlined in white. Her hair stuck out from all directions in a wavy tangle — as if she'd been caught out in a tornado, Wilf thought.

"How chic!" exclaimed Wilf's mother.

"Wait. I don't have my warts yet." Morticia took off in the direction of the kitchen.

"Warts?" asked Wilf's father, still holding the jagged pieces of newspaper.

"Raisins," said Wilf's mother. "She glues them on."

"Oh."

The doorbell rang.

"That's Kathlyn!" yelled Morticia. "Let her in."

But it was Chuckie.

"Hi, Chuckie," said Wilf's mother. "I thought Wilf said you weren't going to the dance."

"Not with a date, Mrs. Farkus. I'm on the food committee. I have to keep the punch bowl filled. It'll be boring, I'm sure, but at least I'll be there. Wilf's the lucky one. Boy, I bet he's going to have lots to tell you when he gets home. He'll probably chew your ears —"

"Let's go," said Wilf, grabbing Chuckie's arm. "We don't want to be late."

Before they could get to the door, however, the bell rang again.

"That's Kathlyn!" yelled Morticia automatically. She reappeared from the kitchen. Three black lumps stuck out from her chin, her nose, and her forehead.

This time, it *was* Kathlyn, who, although a witch, too, was a much more traditional type. She was carrying a stuffed cat with a red bow tied around its neck and wore a pointy witch hat over her short blond hair.

Wilf picked up the small plastic box that held Heather's daisies from the hall table, tucked it under his arm, and pushed Chuckie out the door. But as soon as he shut it, it opened again.

"We'll walk you as far as Heather's house," Morticia said. "We want to see what kind of a dress she's wearing."

128 •

Wilf looked at Chuckie in desperation. How was he going to cut through lawns and change clothes with the other Wilf with Morticia dogging his every step? Chuckie shrugged and kept moving. The girls walked up ahead. Wilf could hear Morticia complaining for the hundred and fiftieth time that she had impossibly antique parents who wouldn't let her ride in Todd Carmichael's car. Wilf's thoughts churned as they neared the corner of Greenwood. Then, just as they were passing the Colbys' house, which he often used as a shortcut to the Day 'n Night Supermarket, Wilf took the corsage box from under his arm and tossed it behind a nearby hedge.

"Oh, no!" he cried.

Morticia stopped. "What's the matter?"

"Heather's flowers. I forgot them. I have to go back."

"Gosh, you don't want to ruin the whole night before the dance even starts," Chuckie said. "Go ahead. I'll wait for you."

Wilf ran to the side of the Colbys' garage, then paused to listen. Chuckie was trying to convince Morticia that Wilf didn't need his sister hanging around on his very first date. He wasn't having much success until Kathlyn broke in and said that since one of their big scenes was right at the beginning of the play, they'd better not wait any longer or Mr. Pauly would probably just go on without them.

Morticia pouted. "Wouldn't it be just like him."

"We can sneak into the cafeteria after rehearsal's over," Kathlyn suggested. "Maybe we can even get your brother to do his funky dance."

At last Morticia gave in, and the two girls left. Wilf wiped the sweat off his forehead and headed toward his garage.

The other Wilf had his head inside the family sedan and was fiddling with the knobs and buttons on the dashboard. The headlights flashed on and off a couple of times before Wilf pulled him away.

"Quick. We don't have much time."

"Hey, nice outfit," said the other Wilf, looking admiringly at Wilf's navy-blue baggy pants and off-white shirt with the thin blue stripes.

In a few minutes, the switch was complete. Wilf, back in his jeans and white T-shirt, looked at the other Wilf in his new clothes and agreed with his mother. He did look handsome. Or he *had* looked handsome. Whatever.

"Are you sure you want me to do this?" asked the other Wilf.

"I'm sure. Now move, will you? Chuckie's waiting over on Greenwood," Wilf said. "Have a good time." He was sounding like a parent again.

The other Wilf started to go, then turned back. "I feel bad that I'm going to have one and you aren't," he said.

130 •

"One what?"

"Good time. It would be neat if we both could go."

For a minute, Wilf could almost picture it. Then, "Don't worry about me," he said brusquely, shutting out the scene.

"But you'll be all alone."

"Yeah, well, that's my choice."

The other Wilf stood there for a minute.

Wilf heard the bang of a screen door. "My parents are coming! Scram!"

The other Wilf disappeared. Wilf himself got out of the garage just in time. The garage door went up, and his father's voice came from close by.

"Please stop sniffling, Rosemary. It's just a junior-high dance, not a ten-year polar expedition. And may I remind you that you were the one who was so insistent upon his going."

"It's a mother's prerogative to cry at milestones in her children's lives. You men put on this big show like you don't have any emotions. I can't wait to see you walk your daughter down the aisle."

His father's reply was lost in the slam of the car door. Wilf crouched low in the grass behind the garage. Minutes later, the car backed down the drive and out onto the street. Wilf waited awhile, then crept across the backyard and into the house.

He wandered aimlessly through the empty rooms while the sun dipped lower and lower. Here he was, alone again, just like the boy mummy in the pyramid. Having a clone to do all the things you didn't want to do had seemed like a great idea. But it hadn't turned out quite the way he'd expected. It occurred to him, now that he thought about it, that a robot would definitely be much better. It would just be a piece of machinery. It couldn't take over your whole existence.

Except he didn't have a robot. And he couldn't afford to wait until the next century for somebody to invent one. If the other Wilf had never hatched out of that OceanPups egg, he, Wilf, would still be getting D's and hooks on his report card. He'd still be grounded. And he'd still feel like a wildebeest in school. At least now the other kids noticed him, even if it wasn't really him.

Wilf was suddenly very tired. On top of the nagging problem of what he was going to do with the other Wilf after next week, it had now struck him that after the other Wilf disappeared, so would his newfound popularity. He'd been relishing the thought that when he got to eighth grade, he'd be the center of attention. But he wouldn't. He didn't know how. If he could only figure out what made the other Wilf so likable . . . It couldn't just be that crazy Farkus Funk. He stared out the window and thought again about being invisible. He imagined himself at the dance, secretly watching the other Wilf in action.

Outside, dusk came slowly creeping along Willowridge Road. Objects began to blur and fade off into shadows. Wilf stared into the murky darkness. People didn't really need to be invisible, did they? All they had to do was stay out of the light. What if . . . ? The idea grew stronger. What if he were to go to the dance? Not inside, naturally. But the cafeteria was on the first floor. And it had windows. Big ones. He could stand safely outside and watch without the slightest danger of being seen!

Hesitating just a moment to quiet a warning voice inside his head, Wilf silently slipped out the back door and through the Colbys' yard.

21

Wilf peered out from behind the trunk of a small tree about ten feet away from the cafeteria windows. From there, he had a pretty good view of almost the entire room, which was strung with loops of red and white crepe-paper streamers and bunches of red and white balloons.

Everyone seemed to be having a good time. A couple of parent chaperones wiggled by, doing what Wilf recognized from *Happy Days* reruns as the twist. Every once in a while, when the crowd parted for a moment, he caught sight of Chuckie behind the refreshment table on the other side of the room. Towering over him was Ellen Anne Vanderhoofft, carefully lining up plastic glasses of punch like numbers in a division problem. He scanned the dancers, focusing in on anything white that could be the other Wilf's shirt. No . . . no . . . no . . . yes! There he was! He seemed to be dancing all alone, but then as Wilf watched, he could see that there were about six girls around him. One of them was Heather Spears-Croxton, looking quite different in her short yellow dress. In his imagination, Wilf had pictured her parading through the school with a "Save the Chipmunks" poster.

"*Mis*-ter Farkus!"

Wilf felt a familiar grip on the back of his shirt, and then he was spun around.

"H-h-hi, Mr. Oldak. S-s-sir," he added through chattering teeth.

"How did you get out here? Didn't I just see you dancing with half the female population of Gatesburg East?"

"Uh — uh, yessir. Yes, I was. You bet!" Wilf tried to squiggle around so Mr. Oldak wasn't facing the cafeteria windows. "I was — uh, it was — well, it was — well, you know — it was, uh, warm."

"So you thought you'd take a little stroll and cool off."

"Eggs-eggs-exactly."

Mr. Oldak released him. "Well, it *is* getting pretty

stuffy in there. But we can't have you kids just wandering around. You may have forgotten, but there's a rule that no student leaves before ten o'clock unless accompanied by a parent. Okay?"

"Yessir, Mr. Oldak." Wilf waited.

"Well?"

Wilf started walking.

"The front door is in the other direction, Mr. Farkus. And when you get in there, please put your shirt back on. I know this affair was advertised as casual dress, but T-shirts are stretching the point."

It's definitely all over now, Wilf thought as he climbed the broad concrete steps. He paused every few seconds and glanced back, hoping that by some miracle Mr. Oldak had been beamed aboard a Zorgonian spaceship. But he hadn't.

Wilf reached the heavy steel doors, pulled one open, and stepped inside the foyer. Up ahead, he could see kids walking through the halls, on their way, he supposed, to and from the lavatories, which were off to the left, away from the cafeteria.

Mrs. Donnally, his science teacher, came toward him. "Oh, hi, Wilf. Have you seen Mr. Oldak?" she asked.

Wilf nodded and pointed toward the door.

"Thanks." She smiled. "They're having a little problem with one of the loudspeakers for the sound system, and he seems to be the only one around who understands these things. We wouldn't want the music to go dead on us before we get to see your exhibition, would we?"

Exhibition?

Mrs. Donnally went out the door, but Wilf knew both she and Mr. Oldak would be coming back shortly. No one else had noticed him. Yet. Maybe he still had a chance. If somehow he could get to an empty classroom and hide . . .

Wilf edged his way along the wall. Suddenly, just before he reached the main hallway, he caught sight of the other Wilf. He was heading in the direction of the boys' lav. This could be the opportunity he was looking for! Once the other Wilf was safely out of sight, Wilf himself might possibly risk showing his face for a minute or two. Okay. Now. Slowly, slowly. He eased out into the hall, where Marilee Manzetti promptly pounced on him.

"Come on! We're waiting for you! What did you do with your shirt?"

"I —" he began, but Marilee apparently wasn't interested in an answer. He had no choice but to let her lead him toward the bright lights of the cafeteria, then through the jostling crowd to the small circle of girls who stood around Heather Spears-Croxton like petals on a flower.

"Wilf! You're back!" they chorused.

Hands thrust him forward, and then he was surrounded by an army of girls who were twitching around like they'd caught poison ivy. He stood there, feeling as if he had two left feet. No, six left feet. And all of them were nailed to the floor. But he had to try. One by one, he picked up his sneakers and put them down. Self-consciously, he glanced at the other boys on the dance floor. He didn't seem to be doing anything different.

Then, all at once, he found himself caught up in the music. He was dancing!

Heather wiggled over until she was right beside him. "You were really a scream with Andrea Carlucci's cousin in Life Skills this morning."

Wilf knew who Andrea Carlucci was. What was this about a cousin? And what had been so funny? His concentration slipped. He felt his heel come down on something soft.

"*Ow!*"

"Sorry."

"When you started to put that diaper on his *head* —" Heather went on.

Marilee piped up, "Miss Skolnik said she couldn't believe you'd never seen a baby before in your life."

Wilf shuffled his way over toward Darcie Bell and away from any more talk about babies. Darcie smiled at him. He smiled back. Out of the corner of his eye, he could see Heather flash him an annoyed look, so he moved on to Nanci Hanley. She smiled at him, too. He was beginning to really enjoy himself — so much so that he almost forgot about the other Wilf, until he happened to look over and see Chuckie behind the refreshment table and panicked.

Wilf heard someone cry, "Where are you going?" as he turned and shot through the crowd. "Thirsty!" he called back over his shoulder. Reaching the table, he grabbed a plastic cup from Ellen Anne's division problem, tossed down the purplish liquid in one gulp, then leaned over and whispered desperately to Chuckie: "I need you."

"In a minute." Chuckie was swirling a ladle around in the punch bowl, trying to catch a magenta orange slice.

Wilf stuck his hand in the punch, plucked the orange slice out, and plopped it into Chuckie's hand.

"Hey!"

"*Now.*"

"Hold your horses, will you, Wilf? I have to get some more cups."

Chuckie vanished below the edge of the table. Wilf dropped to his knees and stuck his head under the white paper tablecloth. "Chuckie, look at me! I'm the *real* Wilf!"

In the semidark, Chuckie's eyes glowed round.

"He's in the lav! Quick, Chuckie! You've got to go and tell him to stay there!"

Chuckie didn't wait to ask any more questions.

The tablecloth rustled. "What's the matter?" Heather Spears-Croxton had crawled halfway under the table beside him.

"I — I dropped something." Wilf started to back out.

"Did you find it?"

"Uh, yeah, I did." He got to his feet, only to face Marilee, Nanci, and Darcie. There were smirks on their faces.

"What were you and Heather doing under there alone?" Marilee asked.

"Together," added Nanci.

Wilf felt his cheeks growing warm. Then, suddenly, across the room, Chuckie appeared at the cafeteria door. He was waving his arms as if he was parking a jet airplane.

"I have to go," Wilf said.

"Where?" asked Heather.

"Uh, to the lav."

"Again?"

"Too much punch," Marilee offered. "But don't forget it's almost nine-thirty."

What was going to happen at nine-thirty? Wilf wondered as he wove his way through the crowd.

"He wants to see you," Chuckie hissed when Wilf joined him.

"Where is he?"

"Still in there, of course." Chuckie jerked his thumb

in the direction of the lav. "Where'd you think? The principal's office?"

Chuckie sounded grouchy. Wilf continued down the hall. He pushed open the door marked BOYS and went in. The place was empty. There weren't even any shoes showing from beneath either of the two partitions. Puzzled, Wilf tried to think what to do. The next minute he found himself being pulled inside a stall. The other Wilf was standing above him on the toilet seat.

"What are you *doing?*" hissed Wilf, frantic.

"What are *you* doing?" the other Wilf hissed back. "You're supposed to be home."

"Well, I —" began Wilf, but he was interrupted by the sound of someone entering the lav.

"Wilf? Wilf Farkus?"

Wilf's voice froze in his throat.

"I'm in here," called out the other Wilf.

"Oh. Sorry to bother you. It's Ray Oldak. Mrs. Donnally sent me in to see if you were ready to do your thing. We got the bugs out of the sound system."

"I'll be right there, Mr. Oldak."

As soon as the door wheezed shut, Wilf said, "What 'thing' is he talking about?"

"The Farkus Funk. Everybody wants to learn it," the other Wilf said. "So I promised to teach them. Unless, that is, you'd care to take my place."

"Maybe I will," returned Wilf, defiantly. "I can dance, too, you know."

"Okay, go ahead."

"What are you going to do?"

"Me? Come out and boogie along."

"You wouldn't dare."

"Why not? This whole stand-in idea was something you cooked up to get yourself out of trouble. Now, just because I'm doing a better job at being you than you are, you're ready to get rid of me. I figure I might as well stick around and take my final bow."

Wilf gulped. "What makes you think I want to get rid of you?"

"Oh, just this picture that keeps running through my head where I'm lost in a big building with lots of stores."

Had Chuckie gone and told the other Wilf about the mall? Or had he been reading Wilf's mind again? No, that wasn't possible. There wasn't any such thing as mind reading. Or was there? "Getting lost would be better than getting dissected," Wilf reminded him.

"Watch how scared I am." Without another word, the other Wilf jumped off the toilet seat, pushed past Wilf, and went out into the hall.

Wilf started to follow, then stopped. If he blew the whistle now, the world would know he had a clone. They both would be labeled freaks, which was definitely worse than being a wildebeest. And the government would probably end up dissecting them, too. Not that Wilf cared about the other Wilf. He wasn't real. But Wilf was worried, too, about what his parents would think when they found out that he'd kept the other Wilf a secret. They'd also be pretty upset at what he'd done. His father would not only consider him lazy, but a liar and cheat as well.

This time Wilf didn't have to worry about being seen. The halls were empty. When he reached the foyer, Wilf glanced back toward the cafeteria. The entire seventh-grade class, the parent chaperones, and the teachers were lined up in rows like a gymnastics class. Front and center stood the other Wilf, leading them all through the steps of the Farkus Funk. Not even one head turned in Wilf's direction.

The lights were on at 218 Willowridge. His parents were home. They'd be waiting up for him. No, not for him. For the other Wilf. The Wilf everyone liked. Even Chuckie. He, the real Wilf, didn't know who he was anymore. Again he wished he could go in the house and tell his parents everything. But he was in too deep. There was only one thing to do now. He would go away. Then everyone would be happy.

Wilf paced up and down the driveway, trying to fig-ure out where he could go. Besides the mall, that was. As he neared the garage, he heard the scuff of a shoe on the pavement nearby. He wheeled around, but not fast enough. A rough, smelly bag came down over his head. He tried to yell, but a hand pressed hard against his mouth and he was lifted off his feet.

22

The bag was scratchy against his skin and reeked of something rotten, like — like — like moldy potatoes, Wilf decided with a small sense of relief. For the past several minutes he'd been trying to focus on some little thing in the hopes of forgetting how terrified he was.

He was squashed between two bodies in the front seat of some kind of car. He could hardly move. His hands and feet were tied, not with ropes, but with what felt like strips of cloth. He could feel the motion of the driver maneuvering the steering wheel.

Who were these people? He guessed they were kidnappers. But why had they taken *him?* His mother and father didn't have any money. It would have made some sense if their pictures had been in the paper for winning the *Reader's Digest* Sweepstakes and could have sold a Porsche or two for the ransom. But there was no way his parents would be able to buy him back, even if they wanted to. They might not even realize that he was gone, unless Chuckie told them what had happened, and lately Chuckie seemed to have forgotten that he'd ever smeared Wilf's face with finger paints in the Little Lamb Nursery School. He, the real Wilf, probably wouldn't even get his picture on a milk carton.

The vehicle drove on, turning a corner every so often, here and there coming to a halt at what Wilf guessed might have been red lights. The continual stopping and starting made him think that they were still in Gatesburg. Exactly where, he had no idea.

Soon after the car had pulled away down Willowridge Road, the hand over his mouth had been replaced by another strip of cloth. He'd tried to wriggle free, but a powerful hand grasped his right leg so hard Wilf thought he'd have dents for the rest of his life. However long that was going to be.

Fear clutched at Wilf's insides like a dog gnawing at a bone. Just a few months ago, he'd thought that school was the worst thing that could happen to him. A tear trickled down his cheek and was absorbed by the rough burlap. Quite a few others followed.

The car swerved and went over a bump. The sounds of other traffic faded away. The engine roared briefly in what seemed to be a very large, empty space, then was shut off. Wilf began to struggle again. This time no one stopped him. He heard the car doors open, and then he was pulled out and thrown over a strong shoulder. A few minutes later, he was set gently down on a hard wooden chair. Hands fumbled with the burlap bag. Soon his head was free. He breathed in deeply to get rid of the rotten potato smell in his nose and blinked his eyes.

When his vision adjusted to the light, Wilf saw that he was in a small room, with a dusty desk that held only a dim lamp. Two men stood over him. To his relief, they didn't look very menacing. In fact, Wilf got the strange idea that they were actually very glad to see him.

"I w-want to go home," was all he could get out. He didn't care if his parents grounded him until *3015,* if only he could just see them again.

"All in good time, son," the shorter of the two said soothingly. He was dressed in a dark brown suit and his shoes had been buffed to a deep shine. If Wilf had seen him walking down the street, he would have thought he was an ordinary businessman. "But don't be concerned. We aren't going to hurt you. Why, that's the furthest thing from our minds — isn't that right, Conrad?"

The man called Conrad was thin and scrawny. A baggy tan sweater hung almost to his knees over a pair of faded jeans. He was staring at Wilf with pale eyes and nodding his mop of dirty brownish-gray hair vigorously up and down. Without taking his eyes off Wilf, he repeated, "Right."

Both men's voices seemed somewhat familiar.

"He's beautiful, Victor!" Conrad blurted out suddenly. "They said I couldn't make a clone, but —"

Suddenly Wilf knew. "You — you're from The Impossibility Company!"

Victor smiled. "Exactly. So now we're sure of one thing, aren't we?" He turned to Conrad, who looked blank. "This isn't the one we're most interested in. Oh, not to worry," he added as Conrad's face fell. "We'll eventually need to get them both, anyway." He turned to Wilf. "If this young man will just kindly tell us where his twin is, then we can pick him up."

It was a good thing Wilf's brain had been resting for the past two weeks, because he needed it now more than ever. What was he going to do? He had been very careful not to let anyone see him and the other Wilf together. He didn't think Victor could really be sure that the other Wilf even existed. "I don't know what you're talking about," he lied, for once not caring if he *did* sound like the *Weekly Screamer*. "I don't have a twin. I don't even have a dog. Ask my mother and father. There's just my sister and —"

Victor waved his hand. "Yes, yes, we know all about your family, Mr. Wilfred D. Farkus. We've been watching you all for the past two weeks from our truck."

The black pickup! Those were Conrad's strange, pale eyes that had stared out from the truck the day he'd helped his father drag the mattresses out to the curb. "I told you —"

"— that you don't have a twin. I know. Technically, that's true. The letters T.W.I.N. are the hallmark of our company, Conrad's and mine. It's an acronym for Transferable Wonders, Inc. You see, Conrad is a brilliant geneticist."

Conrad nodded solemnly.

"We both used to work for the government. I basically shuffled papers around. Conrad, however, conducted actual experiments. One of them was to create a featherless chicken that would produce more meat. Right away I realized his great potential." Victor took out a handkerchief and wiped the dusty desk clean, then hiked himself up onto one corner of it.

Wilf relaxed a little. He felt as if he was back in school, with Mrs. Donnally droning on and on about how there were over two hundred bones in the human skeleton. Actually, Victor was much more interesting than Mrs. Donnally. Wilf wondered if he'd ever thought of becoming a teacher instead of a kidnapper.

"Conrad's cloning experiments were limited to plants and some lower forms of animal life. Science, it seems, is reluctant to experiment on humans." Victor eased off the desk and began pacing back and forth. "Just think of what clones will mean to society, young man! Never again will doctors have to concern themselves with artificial hearts or bionic limbs, or finding compatible donors for transfusions! A person's clone will be a genetic duplicate. It will automatically provide, without any fear of rejection, any part of the body that has worn out or ceased to function. Why, it's like giving the world the Fountain of Youth!"

Conrad's eyes were glowing. "And Victor helped."

"We decided to set up our own laboratory," Victor went on. "The building we rented had once been a toy novelty company. We found some of these OceanPups kits were still lying around, so we organized The Impossibility Company as a sort of cover. It really was a rather apt description, when you come to think of it."

"But how did I get —" began Wilf, completely forgetting that he denied knowing anything about the other Wilf.

"Your clone? I'm not entirely certain, but I think it may have something to do with the essential nature of scientists. They tend to be somewhat sloppy in their everyday habits. Einstein, for example, was rumored to carry stale sandwiches around in his coat pockets, simply because he'd forgotten to eat. Conrad was not supposed to mix up the OceanPups business with his cloning experiments. But I'm not blaming him for the accident, especially in light of what eventually occurred."

"Accident?"

"Yes. Conrad had been doing some experiments with cows. On the side, he was working with accelerated growth hormones and also preparing OceanPups kits for shipping. I'm afraid he wasn't too careful. A month or so ago, he jarred one of our OceanPups breeding tanks off a shelf. Everything was drenched — order forms, PetPaks, test tubes, petri dishes, and especially the electronic microscope. We salvaged what we could of the mess, dried it all out, and sent out the shipments, but I suspect that's when it happened."

"How did you know where to find me?" asked Wilf.

"We knew that only three kits had been shipped immediately after the accident. One of them was sent back to us because Conrad forgot to put the zip code on the package. The second went to a woman on a ranch in the Midwest. Yours was the third."

Wilf had a dim recollection of some mention of a cow in some lady's kitchen.

"Conrad assumes that a hair or skin cell was in the envelope with your order. That would have been enough. All of your genetic traits would have been contained in it. After your call, we closed up the shop and came to find out if our dream had come true. And now, young man, if you will tell us what we need to know, we'll soon be able to show the world what we have accomplished."

"But you haven't accomplished anything!" Wilf cried. "You said yourself it was an accident!"

"True, but we won't let anyone know that. And we certainly would have proof that it is indeed possible to produce a living clone. I'm sure the government would suddenly become very interested."

Wilf was quiet. What Victor had said about using parts of a clone's body to repair a real person bothered him. He had visions of thousands of clones just sitting around waiting in pens, like featherless chickens.

"I wouldn't hesitate too long, if I were you," said Victor with a mocking smile that caused shivers to run up and down Wilf's back. "We know you have a clone.

You've as much as admitted it. But you obviously haven't told your parents about him, because there would be much more activity around your house than your father cutting the grass. I suspect that for some reason, you're keeping him a secret. Actually, I'm rather glad you did. Now, it would be easier if we could just slip in quietly. However, if we have to search the place and someone gets in the way, there might be trouble. I might warn you, we've gone much too far to let anything stop us now."

All at once Wilf realized that he really wasn't much different from Victor. He'd had the same idea about using a clone. Oh, not for replacing an arm or a leg, but for solving his problems. And now, right or wrong, he must do it again — to save his family.

Wilf gave Victor directions to Gatesburg East Junior High.

23

Victor and Conrad had left, but not before tying Wilf securely to the chair and closing the door. Wilf had heard the distant sound of an engine starting up, and then all was quiet. Very quiet. And very scary.

Wilf felt like he had landed in the middle of a Stephen

King story, although he'd much rather have been reading one. Even *Cujo*. Not that he seemed to be in any immediate danger. At least no snarling dogs were breathing down his neck. But try as he might, he couldn't stop the creepy, crawling sensation from running up and down his arms, and his heart was playing volleyball again inside his chest.

At least Victor hadn't replaced the smelly burlap bag. Wilf was grateful for that. As long as he could use his eyes, he might be able to figure out a way to escape. When the men returned with the other Wilf, they'd both be taken away and probably never heard from again. Chuckie was the only person in the whole world who knew about Wilf's clone. But even if Chuckie told, who would believe him? Nobody, that was who.

He had to get away. They could keep the other Wilf. It would save him the problem of what to do with him later. Oh, sure, maybe he'd miss having a clone a little, especially when his father and mother packed him off to a dumb old private school. But so what? Anything would be better than the mess he was in now.

Wilf began to struggle against the strips of cloth that held him to the chair. At first, they seemed to stretch a little, and he pulled until he thought his hands would come popping off the ends of his arms. Which would have helped in one way, he supposed, but eventually would have caused other problems. So he stopped and tried to think more rationally. Yes, that was it! he thought triumphantly after a minute or two. He could wiggle his chair over to the desk. They were always doing that in adventure movies. And once he reached the desk, he could — he would — what?

Open the drawer, of course. Inside, there might be a scissors, or a knife, or — Wilf's eyes lit on the lamp, which Victor and Conrad had left on. Aha! Even better! He'd just smash the light bulb, and even though it would be dark, he could use the broken glass to cut through the cloth!

Carefully, Wilf began to rock the chair from side to side. It moved an inch. Two inches. Four. Excited, Wilf rocked faster, and suddenly found himself on the floor, eye to eye with a gigantic cockroach. He let out a yell. Even Stephen King couldn't have invented such a horrible sight. Then he noticed that the cockroach was lying on its back with its legs in the air. Its feelers stuck out stiffly and unmoving from its head. Wilf let out a huge sigh. The cockroach sailed across the floor like a dried leaf.

Wilf's shoulder and elbow smarted a little from the fall, but otherwise he seemed to be all in one piece. Far above his head, the lamp burned brightly. How was he going to get to it? He tried butting the desk with his head. It scarcely moved, and after a few more minutes he hadn't accomplished anything except giving himself a headache, so he stopped. It was no use. He felt like crying again, except what good would that do? Wilf rested his aching head on the floor, closed his eyes, and waited for another idea. After a few minutes, he opened his eyes and stared off into space. Then he saw it. Under the desk. A piece of paper. He didn't know how it could help him, but at this point anything was better than nothing. He blew at it. Like the cockroach, it scooted away. Wilf scrunched and wiggled around to the other side of the desk. It seemed to be a small card with printing on it. It was also upside down, but after a few minutes of serious squinting (he'd have to remember to tell Mr. Oldak), Wilf could read it.

"Friendly" Frank Baines: Sales Manager

Gatesburg

1550 Parker Avenue

BLACKJACK MOTORS

For the best deal in cars, it's

Now at least he knew where he was. At least he thought he did. First, he'd had the sense of being in a big, empty place. Then Victor and Conrad had put him in this small office. And all the time he'd been here, there'd been a faint odor of something he'd been too busy to identify. Until now. It was oil.

Once he'd gone with his father to get an oil change

at the place where he'd bought the car. The main show-room had big glass windows where they displayed all the spiffy, most expensive models. The service bay was far in back. Wilf had walked around while his father waited for the man to fill out the paperwork. Along the sides of the bay, mechanics in blue shirts worked on cars.

The words *Blackjack Motors* burned themselves into Wilf's brain. The place obviously wasn't in business any-more, but he wished he was wrong about that and that his father was outside in the customer waiting room, reading a magazine and waiting for his car to be finished. He wished Friendly Frank Baines had forgotten some-thing in his desk drawer when he left and was coming back to get it. He wished Mr. Oldak was there to ask him the date of the First Continental Congress. He even went so far as to wish Cujo Cockroach would wake up.

"Help!" he croaked. But no one answered.

24

He didn't know what time it was. He thought that he might have dozed off, but he wasn't sure. Something had disturbed him. A noise. He looked at Cujo. His legs were still straight up. Wilf listened.

There it was again. His heart almost stopped. The doorknob was slowly turning. Victor and Conrad! As he watched, a crack appeared.

"Доброе утро, мой друг," said a voice.

They had the other Wilf. Now he was really sunk. Even though he knew it was useless, he began to struggle.

"Relax, will you?" said the other Wilf, stepping into the room.

"Re —" began Wilf, then noticed that there was nobody behind the other Wilf. "Where are Victor and Conrad?"

"Who?"

"Never mind! Quick! Untie me. I have to get out of here."

"Hey, buddy, that's what I'm doing. *C'est moi,* to the rescue, as the French say." He grinned. "*Très bien,* eh?"

Wilf felt a surge of hope. He didn't know how the other Wilf had managed to get to Blackjack Motors, but he was relieved to see a familiar face, even if it was his own. Victor and Conrad had obviously missed the other Wilf at the dance. How long it would take them to realize that, he didn't know.

The other Wilf talked while he fumbled with the bands of cloth. "You should have seen it. I had Oldak twisted into a knob."

"Knot," said Wilf automatically.

"Yeah. Well, we were having a great time, but then

suddenly I heard somebody say, 'Blackjack Motors.' "
He paused to pull on one of the bands with his teeth.
"I asked Heather if she was talking to me, but she said
she wasn't talking at all, so I didn't pay any more at-
tention to it. Then it came again. 'Blackjack Motors.'
Also, 'Help!' And something about the First Continental
Congress. But I thought to myself, It's Wilf! He's in
trouble!"

As impossible as it had once seemed, Wilf was now
certain that the other Wilf could somehow read his
mind. There had been the incident on the day of the
thunderstorm, and then again in the Gatesburg East lav,
when the other Wilf let on that he knew about the mall.
Wilf had always wondered if ESP worked both ways.
Maybe, just maybe he'd unconsciously used it to call for
help. If so, it had worked.

"I grabbed Chuckie and told him what I thought,"
the other Wilf was saying. "He said it was pretty weird,
but that a lot of weird stuff had gone on lately and we
couldn't afford to take a chance with his best friend. He
really likes you, Wilf. Anyway, we raced down the hall
to get to a phone and call our father, when who do we
bump into? Allana. Our sister." Wilf didn't bother to
correct the *our's*. "She was with this guy named Todd.
I asked him if he had a car, and he said he did."

The cloths fell from Wilf's wrists. His skin burned.
He rubbed it while the other Wilf began to loosen his
ankles.

"Allana almost had a fit that I wanted to ride in Todd's car, but then Chuckie convinced her it was a real emergency, and so she said she'd better come along."

Any excuse to get a ride with Todd Carmichael herself, thought Wilf. For once, Wilf was thankful for Morticia's freaky behavior. If she hadn't been a witch in the play, she never would have met Todd and he, Wilf, might still be tied up.

"Where are Chuckie and Allana now?" asked Wilf as the last knot parted.

"Todd dropped them off at our house. Chuckie said he'd get help, but I didn't want to wait. We were almost here when Todd's car ran out of food. I ran the rest of the way."

Wilf stood up. His ankles felt like they'd been in a freezer for two months and almost gave out on him, but he shook them and the numbness turned to tingling, which then started to fade. "We have to go," he said. "We're in danger."

"I hear you." The other Wilf made the cutting motion with his hand down his chest. "Dissection?"

"Something like that," said Wilf, moving toward the door. "How did you get in here?"

"Through a place called Customer Service Entrance. I'll show you. All the other doors I tried were locked."

Carefully they crept into the semidarkness outside the room. The other Wilf turned left down a hall, Wilf hanging on to the back of his shirt. They passed another hall going off at a right angle. The smell of oil was even stronger. Then they were in a large, open room. This would be the service bay. There were no cars here now, only a few tire-shaped outlines on the floor and farther back, a yawning black hole that looked like an old grease pit. The squeak of Wilf's sneakers on the cement echoed eerily.

"Over here," said the other Wilf. "Follow me."

They were almost to the pale gray rectangle that spelled freedom when suddenly there was a loud noise. In front of them, a wide door swung up. Bright lights stabbed Wilf's eyes, blinding him. He heard a shout.

"It's the boys! They're both here!"

Wilf shielded his eyes. He could see Victor now, half out of the black pickup. Frantically, he looked around. A low wall stood off to his right.

Wilf wasted no time. He ran across the floor, then vaulted the wall. A second later, he heard a soft thud, as the other Wilf landed beside him. Wilf crouched down. With the lights of the pickup still on, he could see that they were in a room with rows and rows of tall metal shelves. Keeping low, Wilf scooted into the shadowy interior.

"Cut the engine, Conrad!" he heard Victor yell.

Suddenly the air was filled with silence. A few minutes later Wilf heard a nearby scuffing. Paralyzed with fright, he flattened himself behind one of the shelf units and began gnawing on his knuckles. All of them. Something touched his back. He stuffed his hand in his mouth to keep from yelling.

"It's Victor. He came in a side door over there," the other Wilf whispered in his ear. "Come on. Stay down. Let's see if we can get to it."

Shakily, Wilf moved away from his hiding place and followed the other Wilf. Weaving their way in and out of the banks of shelves, they finally made it to the door and through it, into a room filled with filing cabinets and typewriters. From another door in the opposite wall, dim light still poured from Friendly Frank's office. The other Wilf slipped out into a hallway.

"Conrad, head them off!"

Victor's voice was right behind him. Wilf bolted from the room, the *click, click* of an untied sneaker lace sounding in his ears. Well, he sure didn't have time right now to stop and fix it.

Which was a mistake, he realized, as he found himself flying through the air. His mother was always warning him about tripping. He wished he'd listened.

He sprawled face down on the hard floor, sending shock waves up his neck. He shook his head to clear it, then struggled to his hands and knees. In the light that was coming from the hall, he could see a thin, shadowy figure moving toward him. Conrad!

Then, as the man sprang, another shadow dove out of the darkness, wrapped something white around Conrad's face, and spun him crashing into a nearby cardboard display.

"I'll get you a new shirt," the other Wilf paused long enough to say before racing off in the direction of the service bay. But just as he reached it, a pair of arms snaked out from behind a partition and grabbed him.

Wilf, following, looked around frantically. Behind him, Conrad was still disentangling himself from the cardboard. Off to one side, however, another low counter led back to the room with the shelves. Wilf bolted over it, then leaped the half-wall back into the service bay. He sprinted toward the door. The headlights of the black pickup hit him like spotlights on a stage. But neither Victor nor Conrad could stop him now. They were too far behind.

"You realize that he's extinct, don't you?" Victor's voice bellowed out of the darkness, stopping Wilf in his tracks. "If you leave, he buys the farm. Know what that means? Yes, I thought you did. We couldn't afford to let this little episode get out. It would spoil all our future efforts. But go ahead. You don't have to worry. Not really. It's not your life."

Wilf knew he was only seconds from freedom. He turned and yelled defiantly, "Let him go! The cops are coming. I'll tell them all about you and you'll get caught."

Victor chuckled. "That's a dumb trick, especially for a smart kid like you. And even if these imaginary police came, what would you say? That you had a clone, but some big, bad men came and kidnapped him?" He laughed. "They'd laugh in your face, Wilfred D. Farkus. But give it a try. Go ahead, walk out of here."

Wilf shut out Victor's mocking voice. He took one tentative step, then stopped, his thoughts continuing to churn. The other Wilf might not be human, any more than Robocop was. He wasn't exactly a brine shrimp either, but he *was* alive. Although maybe not much longer. And Wilf, whether he'd meant to or not, had somehow been responsible for his being. Did it really make a difference if a living thing hatched from an egg? Having the other Wilf around had added something special to Wilf's days. Something that no one else in the world had. And even though Wilf had often wished he'd never heard the word *clone,* the other Wilf had risked whatever kind of existence he had to come to Wilf's rescue. Wilf knew that he couldn't walk out on him now.

25

"We did well, Conrad," Victor said as Wilf walked slowly back. Victor had the other Wilf's arms pinned to his sides. "Our little specimen has a good head on his shoulders."

Wilf promised himself that if he ever got back to Gatesburg East Junior High in one piece, he'd never again complain about homework or report cards or even detention. He'd bury himself in books, just like Ellen Anne Vanderhoofft. He'd get a 110 average every marking period, and not just in math.

Conrad didn't seem to be too interested in what Victor was saying. He kept looking from one Wilf to the other and getting more and more excited. Finally, he couldn't hold it in any longer. "They're perfect! You can't tell them apart. Look! They even have identical moles on their necks!"

"Unfortunately, we don't have time for detailed observation at this point," interrupted Victor. "There's a small chance that someone will be missing our young Mr. Farkus, so I suggest we all get in the truck and just drive quietly away."

Wilf was thinking furiously as Victor began to tie the other Wilf's hands together. Conrad stood by, impatiently flipping the keys to the pickup up into the air and catching them again. Once he missed, and the keys fell to the cement floor with a clatter. Wilf glanced down, and as he did so, a saying sprang into his mind.

"When in trouble, it is sometimes wiser to use feet than brains."

He recognized the words. They were from the other

Wilf's fortune cookie. And right now they made sense. Good sense. If only he could . . . He still wasn't a hundred percent sure that it would work. He thought maybe he'd done it earlier when he'd unconsciously sent out a call for help. This time it would be for real. It was the only chance they had left.

Squeezing his eyes shut, Wilf concentrated on sending a message to the other Wilf's brain. Aim for Victor's shin, Wilf! Kick it hard! Ready? On the count of three! One, two —

Wilf's own foot exploded outward and connected with the solid bone of Conrad's leg. For a minute, he thought he'd broken his big toe. Conrad grabbed his ankle with both hands, grimacing in pain. Quickly, Wilf shoved him while he was off balance. Conrad dropped to the floor.

Wilf spun around and saw Victor dancing a jig. The other Wilf was nowhere in sight. Before Wilf could move, however, he came shooting out from behind the service counter on a strange-looking square board. It looked almost — but it couldn't be!

With one smooth maneuver, the other Wilf sideswiped Conrad, who had been struggling to get to his feet. "Skateboarding!" he crowed as Conrad went down again. "I learned it from Scuzzy Shusterman after school one day. Hop on!"

It wasn't a skateboard, of course, Wilf realized as he leaped aboard and started to pump. It was one of those

dollies that mechanics use when they need to get at things on the undersides of cars. But it worked on the same principle.

They reached the darkness on the other side of the room. Wilf jumped off.

"What are you doing, man?" whispered the other Wilf, skidding to a stop. "We have to get out of here."

Wilf held up his hand. "Listen! A siren!"

The other Wilf cocked his head.

"I don't think Victor's heard it yet," Wilf said. "All we have to do is keep him occupied for a few minutes. Then when the cops arrive, we sneak out the door, and they'll at least get nabbed for breaking and entering."

"Молодец!" the other Wilf said admiringly. He swung the dolly around and charged off again into the light. Victor was moving toward Wilf. The other Wilf circled around and came up behind him, running the dolly up his heel. Wilf had accidentally done the same thing to his mother once or twice in the Day 'n Night Supermarket when he'd gotten too close with the grocery cart.

Victor cursed and swung around, limping. The other Wilf had zoomed off to the back of the service bay and was practicing a few flips. As Wilf watched, holding his breath, the other Wilf executed a perfect 360-degree turn on the edge of the old grease pit.

With a roar, Victor rushed at him. The other Wilf

stepped on the back of the dolly, prepared to maneuver out of the way. Victor launched himself through the air. There seemed to be a wild confusion of arms, legs, and heads. Then Wilf heard a frantic-sounding "*Noooooo!*" followed by a thud.

The siren was louder now. Conrad, who was opening the door to the pickup, heard it, too. Wilf acted fast. Bending down, he grabbed a dusty tire off the floor and with a mighty shove sent it spinning across the floor. It caught Conrad square behind the knees.

A flash of red lit up the darkness outside. The other Wilf had disappeared. Wilf was just heading toward the grease pit in the hopes of finding him when what sounded like a wildebeest migration came pounding into the service bay.

"Just what the hell is going on here?"

Wilf didn't have to turn around to recognize that voice. But then he did, and saw not only his father but also his mother, Chuckie, Morticia, and a boy in black tights that Wilf assumed was Todd Carmichael, alias Macbeth. They were staring. Wilf supposed he couldn't blame them.

"Hi, Dad," he said weakly.

Suddenly, from out of the darkness, the other Wilf appeared, his face smudged with black. "Yeah, hi, Dad."

"Dad, do you remember that cryptobiosis I was telling you about?" Wilf began cautiously, and went on for several minutes while the police were busy handcuffing Conrad and getting Victor out of the grease pit. When he reached the part about finding the other Wilf in the bathroom, he stopped, worried. His father hadn't moved. Not even his eyeballs, which remained glued on the other Wilf. Wilf supposed it was a natural reaction, but still . . .

"Mr. Farkus? Sir?"

A heavyset man in a dark suit came out of the shadows. He was tucking a small notebook into a pocket inside his coat. Wilf's father acted like he didn't even see him.

"Mr. Farkus? Detective Broncato. Sir, I know it's late, but we'd really appreciate it if you and your sons could come down to the station for a few minutes to answer some questions. Sir?" He glanced at Wilf. "Is he all right?"

"Dad!" Wilf said.

His father drew a deep breath and held it until Wilf thought he was going to turn blue. His body shuddered, sort of like a dog shaking off water, Wilf thought. Then slowly his head turned toward the detective. "S-s-sons?"

"Your boys, sir. The twins there." He pointed at the two Wilfs. "They *are* yours, aren't they?"

"We sure are!" Quickly Wilf threw one arm around the other Wilf and the other around his father's waist. He smiled at Detective Broncato. "I'm Wilf and he's — uh — he's . . ."

"Steve," supplied the other Wilf.

168 •

"Steve?" asked Wilf, startled.

The other Wilf shrugged.

Wilf hurried on. "Most people think we take after the Farkus side of the family, but actually my mother — that's her" — he pointed — "my mother says —"

"Wilf, be quiet," ordered a firm voice beside him. Wilf peered at his father. He seemed to have come out of his trance, or whatever it had been. Only one muscle at the corner of his cheek near his ear twitched now and then.

"Now, Officer —"

"Detective," said Detective Broncato.

"Detective, then," corrected Wilf's father. "My — er, my —"

Morticia materialized from behind them. Slowly she walked up and pointed a three-inch-long black fingernail. "Dad, there's —"

"Is this your daughter?" asked Detective Broncato. Wilf couldn't tell if he meant did Morticia belong to the Farkus family or was she a girl. Sometimes he asked himself the same questions.

"Allana," Wilf's father said, "get in the car."

As confused as she appeared, Morticia made time for a quick head count. "There's too many people," she announced. "There's Mom and Chuckie and —" She looked at the other Wilf and forgot what she was saying.

"Get that other kid — the one in the funny clothes — to take you, then."

"He's Macbeth."

"I don't care if he's Julius Caesar. Just tell him to drive carefully and go straight home or you might as well forget that Henry Ford even invented automobiles."

Morticia didn't need another invitation. She grabbed Todd Carmichael by the hand and dragged him out of Blackjack Motors.

"About the station —" began Detective Broncato.

"The — er, the boys have been through enough for one night," Wilf's father said. "Tomorrow will be sufficient. *Tomorrow*," he repeated as the detective opened his mouth to protest. "I'll get your mother," he said to Wilf. "You bring Chuckie and — and *him*." He waved toward the other Wilf, who was grinning and whipping his head back and forth in time to the rhythm of the red light on the top of the patrol car outside.

"Come on, Steve," Wilf said. "We're going home."

26

In the morning, Wilf found his mother sitting on a step at the bottom of the stairs, gnawing on a stalk of celery. On her knees was a plate containing four cold Buffalo-style chicken wings, a half-empty container of blue cheese dip, and a mound of bones. From the kitchen, he could hear the low rumbling of his father's voice as he talked on the telephone.

Wilf sat down beside his mother, absently picked up a chicken wing, and bit it. His mother turned and looked at him. A puzzled line appeared on her brow.

"I'm Wilf," Wilf said hastily.

"Oh. Well, where's —"

"Still asleep. So is Allana."

"Oh," she said again.

They sat there in silence. After a few minutes, Wilf felt his mother's arm slip across his shoulders, drawing him close.

As soon as they had arrived home the night before, Wilf's father called a family meeting in the living room and asked Wilf to tell his story from the beginning. So he did — about how lost he had felt at school, about his idea of growing the OceanPups for a science project, about the sudden appearance of the other Wilf in the bathroom, about his idea of sending him to school in his place, about Conrad's strange pale eyes staring out at him from the black pickup, about Heather Spears-Croxton and how he hadn't wanted to go to the seventh-grade dance, about the moldy potato smell of the burlap bag, about what Victor had said, and then, just as he was about to run out of breath, about the escape at Blackjack Motors.

"Wilf," said his father in growing disbelief.

"Dad —"

"*Wilf!*"

"It's *true,* Dad!" Wilf cried, on the verge of tears. "I'm not making it up. Ask Chuckie. He was here. He'll tell you."

His father moaned and ran his fingers through his hair. "Who else knows about this?"

"Nobody. Just Chuckie," said Wilf.

Morticia fought back a yawn. "Don't forget Todd," she said, and picked a black raisin wart off her chin.

"Plus the entire Gatesburg police force," added Wilf's mother, speaking for the first time since she'd seen the oth — Steve.

"But Chuckie's the only one who knows what really happened," protested Wilf.

"Let's hope it stays that way," said his father fervently. "All right. Suppose, just for the moment, that this is real, and not somebody's ridiculous idea of a practical joke." He glanced at his watch. "It's after midnight. I can't deal with this right now. Why don't we all go to bed and sleep on it."

Wilf's mother flashed him a look that said she doubted if she'd be doing much sleeping for quite some time.

Wilf's father came out of the kitchen, rubbing the side of his head. "It's a good thing your sister works for a congressman. I can't imagine trying to handle all that bureaucratic red tape on my own."

"What does George Honeycutt have to do with this?" asked Wilf's mother.

"Well, I thought the logical thing would be to contact someone in the government. I figured Honeycutt might be able to pull some strings. I had to tread pretty carefully, though. I just said I needed to talk to someone about an urgent medical matter that might have security implications. I could tell he was dying of curiosity, but he was nice enough not to ask. He suggested I get in touch with a Dr. Lipani at the Bureau of Scientific Research and Development. I got switched to a dozen different departments and put on hold so long that I heard an entire Bach concerto, but I finally reached her."

"And?"

"She was extremely polite. She listened and had a few questions. However, I had the distinct feeling she thought I was your typical kook. I guess I couldn't really blame her. I must have sounded deranged. Anyway, after I finished, she said that teenage boys were often given to peculiar fantasies, and that she wouldn't worry about it too much. She then added that if we ever brought the family to Washington, D.C., she'd be happy to arrange for a personal tour of the White House."

"But didn't you explain . . ." She trailed off.

"I tried, but somehow we got disconnected, and

when I called back, a secretary said that Dr. Lipani was in conference and couldn't be disturbed."

Wilf tried to hide his relief at not being in any imminent danger of dissection.

"You've been watching too many movies," said his father, guessing his thoughts.

"Everything will be all right, Wilf," said his mother. "We'll get it straightened out sooner or later. It's just that having — uh —"

"Steve," supplied Wilf.

"Steve," she repeated. "Right. Anyway, having" — she paused again — "Steve show up has been a pretty big shock for us. Can you understand that?"

Wilf could, having been through a bit of a shock himself these past few weeks. What was even scarier, however, was that his parents, who were supposed to know everything, appeared to be just as stumped as he and Chuckie had been.

"But —" he began.

Wilf's father looked at his wife. "I don't think there's any alternative, is there, Rosemary? No one is ever going to believe us. I don't even want to think about what the police will say this afternoon when we go down to the station. I've about decided not to tell them anything. Steve can just live here with us."

"Al, I know today's women are supposed to be Supermoms," replied Wilf's mother after a moment, "but isn't suddenly showing up with a bouncing teenage son going to raise a few eyebrows?"

Wilf's heart sank. He appreciated their trying to find a nice way to say it, but he knew what the answer was. "Steve can take my place, Mom. He does a lot better than me. He's smart and everybody at school likes him."

"And what do we do with you, pray tell?" asked his father. "Abandon you at the mall?"

Wilf's mother gathered Wilf up and hugged him. "Oh, honey, did you think we liked Steve better? Why, nobody could ever replace you!"

Wilf's father wrapped his long arms around them both. "I swear, I don't know where you get such crazy ideas, Wilf," he said gruffly. "Sure, grades are important, but not as important as being together as a family."

"But Steve doesn't have a family," came Wilf's muffled voice.

"We could work that out somehow. That is, if you think there's room."

Wilf was quiet. Despite everything that had gone wrong, his life had definitely been a lot more exciting since Steve arrived. Maybe he'd proven to himself that he wasn't such a wildebeest. After all, he *had* come up with a pretty unusual plan and managed to carry it off. At least for a while. And he *had* learned how to dance. Maybe it would be nice having a brother. Or whatever. He'd grown accustomed to falling asleep at night with that funny snore/snort echoing in his ears. In fact, maybe he'd get a little peace and quiet, since Morticia would have someone else to bug for a change. And maybe —

there was the stirring of an idea in Wilf's brain — maybe he wouldn't always have to be the one to run to the Day 'n Night Supermarket.

He made up his mind. "There's room," he said.

Later, upstairs, Wilf found Steve still in bed, but awake and staring at the clock on the nightstand.

"How does this thing get its food?" he asked.

Wilf pointed to the plug in the wall. "Electricity. It comes into the house through wires, then goes into the clock and turns some wheels called gears."

Steve picked up Wilf's Walkman from the floor beside the bed. "What about this? There aren't any wires going into the wall."

"That runs on batteries. They make their own electricity. Don't ask me how," Wilf said, seeing another question forming in Steve's eyes. "That's one thing you're going to have to pick up through osmosis." He walked over to his desk, brushed a pile of clothes off the chair so he could sit down, and opened his social studies book.

"What are you doing?"

"Studying."

"Yeah?" Steve bounded out of bed and peered over Wilf's shoulder. "That's a change. Why?"

"Because I have five exams next week. I think I can get through most of them, but Oldak will probably ask all sorts of questions that even the First Continental

Congress wouldn't be able to answer. And if I don't pass, I'm going to end up going to summer school."

"Why can't I just take them for you like you planned?"

"That's not going to work anymore, Steve. As a matter of fact, while I'm trying to cram this stuff into my head, there's a few jobs that have to be done around here."

"Jobs?"

At that moment, Morticia stuck her head in the door. She looked even more frightening in broad daylight. Some of the green had rubbed off her face, but there was still a big streak running diagonally from over her right eye to just below her lip on the left. Her hair — well, Wilf thought a tornado might actually do it some good.

"Just checking," she said after blinking at them for several minutes. Then she shook her head, said, "Weird," and left.

"So does that mean Allana is my sister now, too?" asked Steve.

"I don't think so. You're supposed to be the son of my dad's long-lost brother and his wife who just fell off a mountain in Tanzania." Wilf's eyebrows furrowed. "Let's see. So, if you're Dad's brother's kid, I guess that would make you my cousin."

"Cousin," Steve repeated. "That sounds okay. Yeah. I like that."

Wilf grinned. "Me, too."

*   *   *

In a small cell in the Gatesburg police station, the man named Conrad stretched out on a cot. He looked like he was asleep, but his thoughts were racing. A human clone! Accident or no, he had done what some considered impossible. Only what good was it? No one would ever know. If only Victor hadn't been so greedy, allowing his obsession with money to ruin everything. Science was more important. Now, here he was — a genius, stuck in a musty cell and cheated out of his moment of triumph. It wasn't fair! Somehow he had to find a way to continue with the necessary observation and tests. He needed his freedom. He needed a laboratory. He needed equipment. Most of all, he needed the two boys.

Who could help him get those things? Not Victor. An ambulance had taken him from Blackjack Motors with a broken leg and a possible concussion. (That was lucky. No one had paid any attention to his frenzied raving about clones.) No, certainly not Victor. But there was one person. Someone who believed in his genius. Someone who had tried to talk him out of getting involved with Victor. Someone with powerful connections.

Conrad stood and walked over to the door

of his cell. A guard who was reading a magazine at a desk just outside looked up.

"I want to make a phone call," Conrad said. "They said I was allowed one."

Moments later, he was speaking into a receiver. "Federal Institute of Biomedics? I must talk to Dr. Erdra Lipani. My name is Conrad Mudgett. What? Yes, it's urgent. Tell her it's a matter of life and" — he paused, then chuckled under his breath — "that's all. A matter of life."

WORLDS OF WONDER
FROM
AVON CAMELOT

THE INDIAN IN THE CUPBOARD
Lynne Reid Banks 60012-9/$3.99US/$4.99Can

THE RETURN OF THE INDIAN
Lynne Reid Banks   70284-3/$3.50US only

THE SECRET OF THE INDIAN
Lynne Reid Banks   71040-4/$3.99US only

BEHIND THE ATTIC WALL
Sylvia Cassedy   69843-9/$3.99US/$4.99Can

ALWAYS AND FOREVER FRIENDS
C.S. Adler   70687-3/$3.50US/$4.25Can